ZARA DUSK

Mirror

Contents

Acknowledgement

Massive thanks to my daughter, Lani, whose ideas I steal shamelessly and who makes an excellent sounding board for fixing plot holes (but not the sexy bits!). Thanks also to my son, Sean, for his boundless energy and optimism, and to my amazing husband, Tim, for putting up with all the madness and always encouraging me to follow my passions. You rock!

Thanks also to my biggest fan and loudest advocate, my sister Anne Louise, who motivates me to keep going. To Mum and Dad for their encouragement, to Clare for her feedback on the early drafts, and to all those people out there in internetland who make jolly comments or send lovely emails.

I love youse all.

Scar

Power swells through me as I stride along the wide paving stones of Solren.

I am the Cloaked Queen, the rightful ruler of the Fallen Angels, but they don't recognize my reign. They will never acknowledge a mere mortal as their Queen. I may have the rarest vestigial powers of angels, but I don't have their respect.

The sun is setting in a dramatic display of oranges and pinks, highlighting the tall buildings in the sealed section, some as many as five stories high.

Here under the temperature dome in Solren, the richest of the rich have their homes. Well-dressed gentlemen in the latest fashion with sleeves trailing along the pavers stroll leisurely with all the time in the world. No sprinting to get inside before dusk's end.

Back home in Malanox, time is the one thing nobody has.

My ears prick at the sounds of a fight, which is so uncommon here. A man and a woman emerge from a high-class establishment that I have figured out is like one of the Undercity pleasure hubs, but where the women are paid to take their pleasure.

"You can't say no. I paid you," the man warns, his nose crooked and suit rumpled. "I paid for it, you fucking bitch."

Another well-dressed gentleman scurries past with his head

down, clearly with no intention of intervening in the scuffle that might turn violent. I have a long history with violent scuffles, and this one is teetering right on the edge.

The woman's black hair is long and disheveled, and her voice rises in a shriek. "You never paid for that. I wouldn't do that disgusting thing in a million years."

"You'll do what I tell you." The man slams into the woman, pinning her against a wall so she can't kick. She just beats helplessly on his back.

A familiar heat grows within me, the anger I've been carrying for years and truly nurturing this past month.

Zaden, the Margrave of Malanox, kidnapped me and locked me in his castle. I, like a fool, fell in love with my captor. I believed him when he spoke pretty lies, and he broke my heart when I learned the truth.

But my shining angel, Zaden, betrayed me, and it stung. It fucking stung. He lied about Mom's death, he lied about my sister's death, and he lied about Molly's death.

Since then, I've been tossed between powerful angels, warring males, used as bait and leverage, and I've had enough.

My anger reaches boiling point when I watch this crooked-nosed man use his strength against this tousled woman, pressing her up against the fine gray building, smashing his lips against hers.

"Stop," I command.

The man ignores me. Probably can't hear me above his own squelching kisses. Probably used to tuning out female voices.

I'll give him one more chance. "Stop!"

My voice is louder now, and he can't ignore it.

He turns his neck to look at me. "Wait your turn, love." He looks me up and down, taking in my curves and wild copper hair. "Actually, little love, you can join in now. Wriggle out of those tight black pants and come here."

He crooks a finger at me as though all I want in life is to let his greasy hands grope me.

I scowl. "Not a fucking chance."

He narrows his eyes. "Smile, sweetheart. You want to look pretty, don't you?"

With his other hand, he does something that makes the woman jump and shriek, and the monster in my chest turns feral.

I will teach this disgusting man a lesson.

One month ago, the night I became the Cloaked Queen, I inherited Inflict from the Cloaked King. I stabbed the ruling angel with a celestial-tipped blade and watched him bleed out at my feet, then Inflict moved from his body into mine, completing the dyad.

The dyad, Gaze and Inflict, the two rarest angelic powers, the magic that qualifies me as Queen.

With Gaze, I can see other people's magic, can distinguish powerless humans from those with vestigial magic like me, and can even see angels, who glow as brightly as stars. That brings knowledge.

I've spent the past month practicing and honing my skills, and now I can channel Inflict as easily as breathing.

The crooked-nosed greaseball is still leering at me, practically panting, while fingering the woman behind him. His eyes undress me, coaxing the monster in my chest into life.

Inflict storms from my body, exiting through my feet, and snaking across the paving stones, an indigo-colored arrow of hells below. I send the agony to the man's hand, the one fingering the woman, and when he doubles over, clutching his arm, I finally grin.

"You're right. It does feel good to smile."

He has no clue what's happening and doesn't even know I'm responsible for his agony. This feels good, so good, like vindication for all the sleazebags who've whistled at me over the years. I slowly trace the pain up his arm, down his chest, over his flabby belly, and into his tiny dick.

He falls to the ground, roaring and clutching his groin.

The woman looks from the writhing man to me, her mouth agape, then falls to her knees before me in prayer. "Thank you, angel."

Interesting. Most folks don't believe in angels, but this woman mistakes me for one.

As a girl, I used to sit on the mountain under which my family lived and stare up at Malanox Castle. Even then, it seemed so unfair that the Margrave had so much while the rest of us had so little.

My life's goal was to change all that, to make life fair for the people of Malanox.

Now I know there's a whole world of unjust misery outside Malanox, and I want to burn it to the ground.

I will overthrow the Cloaked Council and expose the asshole angels who rule over us. Then every human will believe in angels and understand their malice.

I dismiss the kneeling woman with a wave and continue down the broad street to my hotel.

One of the perks of Inflict is I can get the best room in any inn. If it's a young man with lustful eyes, I usually inflict pleasure. If not, I inflict pain. It doesn't matter to me as long as I have soft furnishings and a large escape window.

Around the corner from my current inn, a bright-white light

glows from an alleyway, marking a hiding angel. I have to move lodgings every few days because the angels find me. If they kill me, they inherit Inflict. They can't get the dyad that way because Gaze is only inherited if I die of natural causes, but most of these bastards will make do with Inflict.

As a bonus, they eliminate the irritating mortal who wields so much power.

Well, if they want to kill me, they'll have to get better at hiding. I daresay half a dozen angels are stashed around here somewhere, but I am not waiting to find out.

I turn on my heel and retrace my steps away from the inn. I cling to the shadows, skulking around like the good old days. I'm sick of watching my back, changing my address, and scanning for enemies.

I can't go home to Malanox—angels will definitely be stationed there waiting for me. But I have to leave Solren.

I know exactly where I need to go, and it's the last place I want to be.

Zaden

A sign swings back and forth in a light breeze, so rusty I can barely make out the picture of the howling cat.

This can't be it. But reliable sources told me I'd find the oracle at the Howling Cat, and I guess this is as good a disguise as any.

I push open the door gingerly so it doesn't fall off its hinges and step into a gloomy, smoke-filled entrance. Beyond a set of insulating hanging ox-hide curtains, the smoke is even thicker, and droning repetitive music is playing from somewhere in the corner.

I've never been in a worse tavern. Half a dozen patrons lounge about, all looking pissed off their tits. One woman with lanky hair and a leather jacket grins at me, and the effort takes her so by surprise she almost topples off her barstool.

She beckons me closer. Every instinct in my body tells me to ignore her, but she looks like a local barfly, so she might know where I can find the Seer.

It's the middle of the day, and we're outside the sealed section of the city, so she's obviously here until dusk. From the looks of her, maybe she sleeps behind the bar.

As soon as I'm close enough, she puts her damp hands on my biceps and squeezes. "You're stacked, even for an angel," she slurs.

That has my attention, and I take in her appearance more closely. Baggy pants with big pockets and even bigger holes showing skinny white legs and lanky brown hair that hangs from her face in greasy strips.

"How do you know I'm an angel? Do you have Gaze?"

I've spent five centuries looking for Gaze. I finally found it in Scarla, but then she walked away, and, for some reason, I let her go. Maybe this greasy-haired barfly could be my ticket to inheriting Gaze from someone else?

The woman shakes her head vigorously, and a greasy string of hair sticks to her cheek. She wipes it away. "Nope, I can just see the things. With my eyes," she slurs, then taps her temple to drive home the point in case I wasn't sure where her eyes were.

Oh, fuck. "Don't tell me you're the Oracle of Howlka," I say on a groan.

"Oh good! I've been trying to get that name to catch on for years! The oracle of the Howling Cat. Howlka, do you get it?"

Maker-be-damned, she is not what I expected. Still, I can see an easy way to get on her good side. I scrape out the stool next to her and sit at the bar. "Can I buy you a drink?"

"You can buy me anything you want," she slurs, leaning against my shoulder, gripping my bicep, and running her fingers along my fitted black shirt. "I mean it. Anything. A new shirt, a drink, a new shirt, one of those tall fancy houses in the sealed section, anything."

"That's very kind of you," I mutter. She's clearly not quite right in the head.

"I'll even let you buy me a kiss," she declares grandiosely.

"Let's start with a drink." I motion the bartender over and order two of whatever the Seer is drinking, which turns out to be a large mug of ale.

"Tastes like piss, doesn't it," she says proudly.

Who knows if she expects me to agree or disagree? I change the subject instead of answering. "I'm looking for something."

She gulps her beer and then nods gravely. "A screw? Because you're the sexiest angel I've ever seen. Tall, muscly, and I'm a sucker for black hair and green eyes. So I'll let you buy me a fuck." She holds up a finger to correct herself. "No, I'll even let *me* buy *you* a fuck."

This is hopeless. I'll come back sometime when she's sober. I slide my ale toward her and stand, but she grips my wrist and locks eyes with me. "Wait, don't go. I know where the Ring is," she says in singsong.

My muscles tighten, and energy thrums through me. "The Ring of Roth?"

She nods gleefully.

I remember nothing from heaven except why I was kicked out. I came to earth and lost the Ring of Roth, and my punishment was to stay here forever.

Actually, it wasn't lost so much as stolen by Elanora, a mortal I fell in love with five-hundred years ago.

I promised myself never to make the same mistake again, the mistake of loving a human. But I did. Scarla became my everything. At first, I wanted to use her for Gaze, with which she can see the gates to return to heaven. Then I fell for her.

She pulled that stupid trick a month ago, killing the Cloaked King and inheriting his Inflict, then telling every fucking angel in Aubia she'd done it and setting a target on her fragile human back.

Then she ran away. I've spent the last month mourning her, fluctuating between boiling anger and empty despair until I realized I could do only one thing.

Instead of finding Scarla, winning Gaze, and sneaking back into heaven, I will find the lost Ring of Roth and perhaps be allowed back in. The Ring directly links to the Elysian plains, which lie outside the gate to heaven. Without the Ring, I cannot return.

But it doesn't follow that with the Ring I'll be allowed in.

I have to ignore all the obstacles to success like the giant burning one—Scarla will never get into heaven because she has committed the greatest sin of all, murder.

The Oracle of Howlka peers at me. "You're thinking of your lover again, aren't you?"

"I don't have a lover," I growl. "Anyway, can you read minds? I thought you could just see the future or something?"

She gives a lopsided shrug. "I just know things. Some future things, some now things."

I grab my mug and take a sip, trying not to wince. "Do you know where the Ring of Roth is?"

"Of course." She hiccups and bashes her flailing hand against her mug, almost toppling it. It rather undermines her authority.

"Where is it?" I grind my teeth, trying to keep patient with this irritating female.

"Don't get pissy with me," she complains, then pats me on the shoulder and gets distracted by my muscles again.

"Please, O Oracle of Howlka, can you tell me where to find the Ring of Roth?"

A smug expression settles over her face, and she deepens her voice, but it still sounds messy and drunk. "To find the Ring of Roth, you must cross the hottest desert, swim the widest ocean, and climb the tallest mountain."

I can't tell if she's taking the piss because that sounds like a load of bullshit, but it's still the best lead I've had in five centuries. "Are you serious?"

The Seer's face is solemn. "An oracle never lies."

Now we're getting somewhere. I know exactly where those places are—the Dead Desert, the Broken Ocean, and the Blue Mountain. They are notoriously dangerous locations, but I am an angel.

I lay a gold coin on the counter and slide it across to the bartender. "Her drinks are on me."

The bartender reaches behind him, opens a cupboard, and pulls out a bottle of fire whiskey and a small shot glass. He pours himself a shot and downs the drink in one gulp. He looks at my generous payment like it's shit and raises his thick furry eyebrows at the oracle.

She reaches across the sticky bar and pats the barman's hand. "There's more coming next time, Oryan, don't worry."

Now I have a plan. I will climb the Blue Mountain, swim the Broken Ocean, cross the Dead Desert, and find the Ring of Roth somewhere along the way. Then, hopefully, the Maker will allow me to return to heaven.

The oracle giggles, and another lanky string of hair sticks to her mouth. "The ring is not your biggest problem, Margrave."

She is an irritating drunk but also the most accurate Seer alive, so I can't afford to ignore anything she says. "What's my biggest problem? The demons from the pit of hells below coming to avenge me for breaking the bloodbond?"

Five hundred years ago, Lord Xerxes helped me alleviate Elanora's suffering by ending her life at my request. I vowed to always take care of his bloodline, and for some stupid reason, I swore it using blood magic.

I kept that vow, even as the generations soured and his

bloodline corrupted. Finally, one descendent, another Lord Xerxes, attacked Scarla, and I lost my mind in a killing haze and sliced him in two, right through his pathetic little heart.

Since then, I've known the demons will come for me eventually; it is only a matter of time.

The oracle giggles like I told her a cracking joke. "No, not the demon either, although it'll be coming for you soon. One shattered bloodbond, one demon to drag your soul to hells below." She waggles a finger at me like I've been a naughty boy. "Nope, your biggest danger is that your lover will die and go to hells, and you'll spend eternity in your dark castle beating yourself up over it." She takes a big swig of ale and wipes her mouth. "Unless the demon gets you first."

I slam my mug on the bar so hard it breaks, and frothy sticky liquid spills across the counter. "Is Scarla in danger? Is she in imminent peril? Or do you mean she'll die eventually at the end of a long life before I lock myself away in misery? If so, that isn't news."

The Seer scratches her nose and nods sagely. "Innimint. In minimint. No, wait, I'll get it...imminent." She smiles proudly.

I jump to my feet, knocking over the bar stool, and sprint to the door.

"See you next time," the Seer shout-slurs, and I blow through the heavy curtains and out the rickety wooden door, which flies off its hinges.

That doesn't matter. Suddenly finding the Ring doesn't even matter. Nothing matters but keeping Scarla safe.

Scar

The streets are empty outside the sealed section of Solren, with the blistering sun high in the sky. Unless they want to be boiled in their skins or frozen solid, folks can only go outside during dawn or dusk. But not me, and not angels. We can go outdoors whenever we like.

I never expected to become the angels' leader, and now that I am, they want me dead. But those assholes rarely leave their elite enclave, so I'm not too worried about running into one out here.

Last night, I slept in a private home, inflicting so much pleasure on the married couple that they were happy to give me their bed while they pleased each other in the other room. I didn't dare stay two nights because they might come to their senses and start asking questions, and I didn't want that kind of attention.

I'm vaguely wandering toward my only friend, Bwadu. She leads the resistance against the angels, living under the rim of the raised city like rats in a hole.

But I can't go there. The very worst move would be to lead a bunch of avenging angels to the den of resistance against them.

But wandering out here gives me time to figure out how to put my plan in motion.

Besides, Bwadu already told me they don't have enough fighters and need more recruits, which dovetails nicely with my escape plan. Now I just need to figure out how to make it happen.

A blur of blinding light flashes out of a tavern and barrels up the street. It is harder to make out the details in broad daylight, but I think I see a tint of purple in that angel's light, and my heart squeezes. Zaden.

But it isn't him. The angelic light burns with yellow like so many of them do.

On a whim, I follow the angel along the cobblestones. He's weaving, drunk, a perfect mark.

He stops at an intersection and leans against a building, catching his breath. I don't bother to muffle my footsteps because his angelic hearing would pick them up anyway.

He smiles when he sees me. "Well, hello, pretty lady."

I scowl. "Oh, you're one of those."

He looks genuinely confused. "One of what?"

"A condescending male who thinks he can dominate a woman through flattery."

The angel's grin widens, showing perfect white teeth. His white hair is pulled back into a braid, with one golden-white ringlet draped over his face. Dark pants and a shirt cover his pale, athletic body, and a whiff of sweet wine fills the air. "Oh, I don't only dominate through flattery, pretty girl." A wicked gleam lights in his eyes.

I'm already sick of him. I inflict him with a light dose of rib pain, nothing too damaging, because I'll need his services.

He frowns at me, not even putting a hand on his chest. "Are you doing that?"

I intensify the pain and smile sweetly. "I'm not just a pretty girl, you know."

This time he clutches his chest. "Fuck-the-Maker, cut it out, would you, little Queen?"

Good. He's figured out who I am, the Cloaked Queen. His Queen.

I release him from his pain. "I'm not a pretty lady, and I'm not a little Queen. Don't ever call me that again."

He grins, mischief sparkling in his eyes. "Okay. You're an enormous, gigantic Queen. In fact, you're so humongous I'm going to call you gigantor. Is that better?"

Despite my best attempt at remaining angry, my lips twitch. "You definitely can't call me gigantor."

He has lightened my mood for the first time in weeks, and I don't feel like killing everyone around me. He should be doubled over in pain and begging or cursing me, but instead, he is joking.

Longing swells in my chest for the banter I used to share with Zaden. I haven't felt that way in a long time, and it's nice to be reminded that my heart and soul are not entirely black.

As a reward, I inflict a pulse of pleasure into the angel.

His eyes widen. "Whoa, you really are the Queen, hey, gigantor?"

I scowl at the name and remove the pleasure. It makes my job easier that he already knows who I am and what I can do, but it's not a good thing that a drunk angel who hangs out outs in dodgy taverns outside the sealed section knows all about me.

That means every angel in Aubia knows about me.

That's a lot of predators.

"What's your name?" I demand.

He sweeps a slight bow, then flicks an errant golden curl behind him. "Lazius, at your service."

"Yes, you are."

He tilts his head. "I'm glad we agree." He points to his chest. "Me, Lazius."

"No, you're at my service." I lace his skin with pain to show him exactly what I mean. "You are in my service until I say otherwise. You will perform tasks for me and do exactly as I say."

His gaze runs down my body. "Tasks?"

I intensify the pain coating his skin. "Not those kinds of tasks."

Lazius seems malleable enough and compliant. Unlike most angels, he has an ounce of personality other than groveling and lying. He'll make a tolerable companion.

"What's my first task?" He leans against the wall again for support, and I wonder how wise it is to choose this angel for my first servant. How long has he been drinking? Is he in any state to carry out my demands?

I sigh. I need to get my plan in motion and can't wait any longer. "I need you to fly me to Desert's Maw."

The city across the Dead Desert is far away from the rule of angels, so I'll be safe there. It also houses a nest of resistance fighters I can recruit to the uprising.

I am their ally, and I recently got a whole lot more powerful.

Lazius slouches and pouts. "Oh, Maker, I don't want to. I'm shit-faced, dude. Let's go tomorrow."

I step closer, so I have to peer up into his face. "Catch me." I leap up, and he grabs me out of the air, holding me like a bride.

"But—"

I encourage him with a dose of pain, and he sighs dramatically and removes the glamor from his wings. They are bright yellow tipped with umber, and just seeing them sends a throb of desire between my thighs, the unfortunate side-effect of being near angel feathers, but I push it away.

"Now," I say warningly.

He sighs dramatically again. "Okay, fine. Whatever you say, gigantor."

He pounds his massive wings, and we rise above the buildings, above the streets, heading north toward Desert's Maw.

Scar

"I can't carry you all the way there, gigantor. My arms will fall off. Actually, I'll probably drop you into the Dead Desert and you'll squish."

We haven't even reached the Maker-be-damned desert yet. We're still flying north from Solren, about to soar over Malanox.

I ping some pain through my captive angel, carefully locating it near his feet so his arms don't spasm open.

He groans. "That doesn't help, you know."

I wish he was lying, but unfortunately, I believe him. When Zaden flew me to Desert's Maw, I was clicked into a harness at his chest.

I sigh dramatically. "Fine. Land in Penngrove Forest, and we'll find something to lash us together."

"Penngrove Forest? We're not all natives of Malanox, you know."

I point to the slash of green beside the castle. "Over there."

Penngrove Forest is too close to Malanox Castle for my liking, and I dread running into Zaden, but we don't have any choice.

We land with a thud, and I zap Lazius with pain.

"Fuck-the-Maker, can you stop inflicting me? I'm taking you to Desert's Maw, so leave me the hells alone."

He slumps to his butt among the moist foliage and leans

against the tree, closing his eyes. I let him rest a few minutes while I pull some vines off a tree and braid them together. It won't be comfortable, but it'll have to do.

A familiar smell snags my attention, and I spy a small clump of Wilton's Dale growing at the base of a yen tree. Its woody stems overflow with pungent needles that can cure the Sighing Sickness.

I must remember this spot so I can come back and pick some Wilton's Dale for the Malanox servants.

No. I shake my head. I'm not that person anymore, the healer who helps. Now I am the Cloaked Queen, with a heart full of vengeance. I push down that tiny part of me that wishes I'd never changed because there is no point in longing for a different past.

I return to Lazius with a makeshift harness and kick him awake. He wipes away his dribble and runs a hand over his braided white-blond hair, then climbs slowly to his feet, grumbling.

"Stand still," I demand, then lash myself to him, my back flush against his chest.

I can't help comparing him to Zaden. Lazius is slightly smaller and paler and smells of stale ale. Not the best comparison.

"Let's go," I bark, pissed that I can't keep Zaden from my thoughts. He lied to me time and again, betrayed me just like everyone else in my life...and even if I could forget all that, we can't be together.

Zaden is fated for heaven, and I am doomed for hell.

"Fine," Lazius grumbles, but he beats his heavy wings and launches us skyward, then north over the desert.

Sunlight burns the red desert floor and reflects so brightly off the sand I have to close my eyes. It was like this last time I crossed. I squeeze my eyes shut but still see the world red and bright.

Hours slip by with the incessant sand sliding by beneath us. At one point, Lazius falters, and we drop twenty feet before I ping him with pain to wake him up.

"Keep it together. We're almost there." I have no idea if that's true, but I need him alert and focused.

"I'm tired," he grumbles, then yawns into my cheek.

I bat away the stench of old ale. "Did you have a bath in beer this morning? You stink."

He reaches down and pokes me in the ribs, hard. "I wasn't expecting to be kidnapped by an evil Queen and forced to do her bidding," he complains.

Fair point. Finally, Desert's Maw becomes a smudge on the horizon then grows into a vibrant city. This city is full of color and sound. With longer dawn and dusk, the streets feel more loved, and it has a thriving outdoor life.

I direct Lazius to land outside The Jagged Tooth, the tavern where I met Bwadu's sister, Mahari. I'm not really here to see her, though. Yes, she runs the resistance in Desert's Maw, so I'll need to contact her eventually, but there's something else I have to do first.

Lazius looks up at the hanging sign of a broken incisor swaying gently above an ox-hide door and doesn't wait for further instructions. He barrels into the tavern but is stopped by a doorman who holds up a hand to bar our way. Tattooed trees grow along his thickly muscled arms. "Pain or pleasure?" His voice is threaded with the harsh, guttural accent of Desert's Maw.

Lazius takes a look around the room. "Just point me toward

some alcohol, buddy."

A smoky warmth fills The Jagged Tooth as we are welcomed by a sultry melody. The tavern has two sections, with a long bar connecting them. On one side of the room are tables scattered about, filled with chattering groups of people. The other half contains two sunken pits, one lined with red rubber and the other with purple velvet.

The doorman lets Lazius pass, then turns to me and repeats his question. "Pain or pleasure?"

Last time I was here, I had no idea what he was talking about. I barely knew about Inflict and definitely didn't know somebody with that rare power operated out of this establishment.

Last time I was here, I was horrified at the concept that anybody would willingly pay good money to experience pain.

Last time, I was a different person.

I look the doorman square in the eyes. "Pain."

"That'll be five gold pieces."

I have no money, but I don't need it anymore. I lean forward and whisper, "And which would you like? Pain or pleasure?"

Something in my manner speaks of strength and power, so the man doesn't challenge me but moves aside and points me toward the pain pit.

The pain pit is lined with red rubber and looks like a blood-soaked mattress. Only one person is in it, his face contorted in agony. Sweat glistens on his brow and cheeks, and his elbows are braced against the rubber.

The air is fetid, choked with the reek of pain and the hint of semen from the pleasure pit.

I look across to Lazius. His pale hands are clasped around a beer, and he's already snoozing with his head on the bar, snoring, somehow staying on the barstool with his long black-clad legs dangling loosely on the carpet. He won't cause any trouble while he's asleep.

He won't be able to kill me. Good.

The Inflictor sits in the same place as last time, on a stool discreetly tucked to one side behind the pits. She's wearing an orange dress and looks bored to tears.

I lock eyes with her. She is a kindred spirit, one of the few people alive who knows what it is to have the burden of Inflict. But her gaze washes over me, disinterested.

I feel hollow at her rejection, even though she has no idea who I am.

My loneliness is complete.

I slide into the pain pit, and friction from the rubber burns my arms. The rubber walls are cold to the touch, dead and ungiving.

I've been betrayed by everybody I've ever cared for. Leo, my childhood best friend, sold me out to Angel VanDyke. Dad lied to me and told me Mom was dead when in fact, she'd abandoned me, abandoned our entire family.

But Zaden's betrayal stings the sharpest. My shining angel, my greatest mistake.

My little loneliness hollows me out, and I watch in anticipation as the whips of vibrant violet magic shoot across the floor, blending in with the vines woven into the carpet, and snake into my pit and into my body.

Blissful agony takes me out of the moment and out of my mind. There is nothing but pain, a sharp stabbing in my internal organs. No thoughts, no self-pity, just torment.

It can't hurt me. Can't cause me actual injury. It just demands the attention of every cell in my body, every thought in my head. It is exactly what I need.

After an eternity, the pain shuts off, and I crumple to the

floor. Rough hands pull me from the pit and drag me across to a booth on the far side of the bar, where patrons drink noisily and everyone stares at me.

"You're cut off," a voice says, dumping me in the booth.

Somebody else slides into the booth across from me and shoves a frothy pink concoction under my nose. "Drink this."

I comply. My dark green shirt is plastered to my body with sweat, and my hair is lank against my scalp. The pain stopped instantly when I was released from those vibrant indigo barbs, but my body still shakes from the aftereffects.

Sipping on the sweet cocktail helps. I come to my senses enough to realize that the person sitting across from me is Mahari.

The woman is black as night and has a warrior's glare. Her thick black hair is shaved on one side of her scalp and left long and flowing on the other. It strikes me again how alike she is to her sister, with the same prominent cheekbones and fuck-off stares.

"What brings you to Desert's Maw?" she asks.

"Oh, just a spot of self-flagellation, you know how it is," I quip.

"It can't just be the pain pit. Surely you can inflict pain on yourself now?"

The world falls into place again, but I feel lighter than before, as though my time in the pain pit was meditative and reset my emotional state. "It isn't the same when I do it to myself."

She sips her drink, which I note isn't frilly and girly like mine but a more respectable whiskey. "Interesting."

I narrow my eyes. "So you know about Inflict?" I keep the question vague and cagey, not wanting to admit I have it. That information is best kept to as few people as possible, as Zaden tried to tell me.

I wish I'd listened. Then I wouldn't have all these angels trying to kill me.

She sips her drink. "Yes. I heard you have the dyad of Inflict and Gaze and are the Cloaked Queen."

I nod, a playful smile twitching on my lips. "Aren't you going to bow for me?"

Mahari raises an eyebrow. "Hardly." She leads the Desert's Maw resistance against the angels, so is unlikely to kowtow to their ruler. "The question is, why aren't you in Solren with all of your fawning celestial subjects?"

I take another sip of my drink. It's sweet and delicious and just what I need. My mood for self-flagellation and disgusting sour whiskeys seems to have passed, and I'm happy to indulge in this nectar. "All of the angels are trying to kill me."

"That one isn't." She hooks a thumb over her finger, and I see Lazius is awake now, watching us through narrowed eyes. He could easily have slaughtered me by now but hasn't. Interesting.

Lazius gives me a little smile and a one-finger salute with a cheeky grin, and I can help smiling back.

Another sip of my girly cocktail lifts my spirits even higher, but I don't understand something. "Hang on, how can you tell he's an angel? You don't have Gaze."

Mahari snorts. "Your arrival wasn't exactly secretive. You literally dropped out of the sky on our doorstep, then menaced your way past Theo. Your angel had barely tucked in his wings before he downed his first shot."

Obviously I need to work on my subterfuge.

"I see you swapped bodyguards. The way your last pet angel looked at you, I thought he'd never let you go. How did you get rid of him?"

Zaden. The male I cannot shake from my thoughts no matter how hard I try. I shrug, trying to pass it off as unimportant, but my voice is strained. "Zaden lied to me about something important. He told me a friend of mine was still alive when she was dead. He could have stepped in and saved her life, but he just let her die."

"Why?"

"Why what?"

"Why did he let her die?"

I twist my fingers in my lap. "Because he was helping me escape from VanDyke's castle."

Mahari laughs. She looks wrong laughing, like a tiger purring. "So this angel chose to save your life over somebody else's, and you're bitching about it? Life's too short, babe. Just get over it. Does he love you?"

That has only one answer. Zaden may have fucked up in an astounding number of ways, but the answer to that question is clear. "Yes."

"And..." She drums her fingers on the wooden table. "Do you love him?"

I stare at her for a few more moments, holding her dark brown gaze. The meditation of pain has sucked away my gloom, leaving me empty and able to examine my emotions for real.

Sure, the string of betrayals from my loved ones still stings, but the one glowing golden globe of light in my chest is due to Zaden. I love him.

I down the rest of my drink and slide out of my chair. "Fuck it."

Mahari grins broadly as I weave around tables and chairs to Lazius. "You have to fly me home to Malanox," I demand.

He grins. "Sure thing, little Queen—"

"Not a little Queen."

"I mean, little gigantor," he slurs. "Climb aboard." He tilts off the bar stool to stand but slips and ends up on the sticky floor. "I'll just finish my nap first," he mumbles, then closes his eyes.

Great. I guess I'll have to find another ride.

Zaden

The Undercity is busy, thronging with people. I push through the second set of heavy ox-hide curtains, and the temperature plummets.

The main cavern is large enough to fit my castle and soars to a peak above. It is lit by flickering torches mounted to each wall. The flames cast a ruddy orange glow across the restless crowd. Smoke from the burning ox fat lingers, making my eyes water and stinging my nostrils.

The steady murmur of conversation, punctuated by the clink of glasses and the crash of plates, echoes across the cavern. A band of musicians plays raucous tunes in the corner, their songs a mix of traditional and modern Undercity melodies, the rhythm infectious and alive.

I seem to have arrived at a mealtime, people thronging everywhere. If Scarla is hiding anywhere, it's here. I lay a slight glamor on myself, enough to avoid attention and help me blend in. Otherwise, my height and frame tend to draw stares.

I stride to the far end of the cavern, scanning every face. A group of men plays dice on a nearby table, their laughter and cheers filling the air.

A small family eats a bowl of gruel sprinkled with blyberries. I never noticed how meager their fare is, but now it seems wrong that these people must eat such tasteless food when I can access every delicious fruit and vegetable available.

Shame coats my skin, raising my temperature. These people are under my dominion, and I could do better by them.

Damn that mortal. She's changed me, changed the very way I see the world. Some of her drive to make people's lives better has rubbed off on me.

I shake my head, trying to clear my thoughts. Finding Scarla is my top priority right now. She isn't in the main cavern, so I head toward the infirmary, down a branching tunnel at the back.

The tunnel broadens and slopes downward, the shadows deepening around me. The walls are slick with moisture, the ceiling low and twisted. A thick musk of sweat and old blood fills the tunnel. It makes my nose wrinkle, but I know this scent well. It is the smell of sickness and recovery, Scarla's specialties. At least, they used to be.

But she isn't in the infirmary either. Although somebody else familiar is here.

I spot Wutan, an angel from Eastern Aubia. He is lanky and bronzed, a slip of a creature almost disappearing into the shadows. His robes rustle like black leaves, dark and mottled.

If angels are here, Scarla isn't.

I turn on my heel and stride, pushing people out of my way, though most give me plenty of space.

Desert's Maw is the only other place I can think she might be. As soon as I set foot into the bright sunshine, I remove the glamor from my wings and pound them, kicking up dirt in my downdraft, and soon I'm soaring north over the Dead Desert.

* * *

27

That drunk Seer, the Oracle of Howlka, told me Scarla's life was in danger and that she would perish if I didn't find her soon.

She might be a drunken wench, but she is also gifted with seeing, so I can't afford to ignore her.

Urgency lends speed to my wings, and I make the trip over the desert in record time and land with a tired thud on the paving stones of Desert's Maw.

I retrace the streets Scarla and I took when we were here together, striding toward The Jagged Tooth. When the tavern is just within view, Scarla barrels out of it like a speeding carriage.

Fuck, she's beautiful. Her copper hair has grown longer in the month since I've seen her and now curls in at her shoulders, growing wilder as it grows longer. She's the only woman I've ever seen with a smattering of freckles, and I love every one of them.

She's tall and strong for a human, strengthened from months of training with me, and I can't drag my eyes away from her long lean muscles or the sway of her hips under those tight black pants as she stalks away. She's wearing a fitted dark green shirt that hugs her breasts and flows in at the waist. Stunning.

But disheveled. Her footsteps are heavy, the stomp of an upset bull. The thump of her heart is the only sound I can hear above my own heart pounding in my ears.

I follow at a distance. Should I approach her and tell her she's in danger? The last time she saw me, she broke my heart and told me we could never be together. Can I handle that rejection again?

I don't know. But I won't let her out of my sight, not while her life is at risk. I cast a glamor over my face so I can get closer, but she's wary of me. She darts a glance my way, and I stop at the intensity of her wide brown eyes.

She frowns, then walks away, increasing her pace.

I don't want her to think I'm the fucking danger. I duck down an alleyway and fly up to the roof of the nearest building. I'll trail her from above if I can't follow her at ground level.

I hop between building roofs, keeping her in sight.

She sticks to the edges of the streets, keeping to the shadows. Her copper hair is like a burst of sunlight among the shadows. Her eyes are bright, alert.

Three men converge on her, and my hand flies to my sword. Ashmodu is always at my hip when I leave the castle, and it buzzes under my grip.

One man lunges at Scarla, and she has to jump away, backing into a narrow laneway with missing cobblestones and a line of trash cans, half of them tipped over, their contents scattered.

The lane is lined by two-story buildings, their doors painted in dull greens and browns, the ox hides rotting and creaking.

Scarla's attacker is tall and thin, with the face of a thug. Thin lips and a long, straight nose, and a thin mustache. He wears a leather jerkin and leather riding boots and stinks of arrogance.

Scarla is a copper blur as she comes up on her toes to dodge his attack. She catches the man's wrist in mid-lunge, twists, and sends him into the nearest wall.

She skilfully unleashes Inflict on them, staring at the men coldly, and all three double over in pain. She's a difficult woman to corner, probably the most powerful human ever.

She moves to exit the laneway, but another two men round the corner and lunge at her, and she's forced back again. These men have swords, so she has to jump further to escape injury, and I have a sinking feeling she's being herded.

Scarla's copper hair flashes like metal shavings as she twists so a sword just misses her throat. She flips into the air, letting the blade whistle past, then comes down with a graceful spin and hits the man's arm. She wraps her hand around the blade, stopping it dead, and then slams her other palm into his forearm, breaking it and forcing the sword clear of its owner.

I shudder as I see the sword sink into the ground, biting into the cobbles two feet deep.

Ahsmodu is vibrating in my hands now, baying for blood, but Scarla is a powerful woman who has it under control. She won't thank me for swooping in when she doesn't need help.

Within another moment, she has the new man under her thrall, writhing under the agony of her Inflict, doubled over on the cobblestones beside his companions. Scarla glances around, searching for more.

She doesn't look up.

More men attack her with swords, and she's forced further down the laneway. Now she's hindered from exiting by the pile of bodies on the floor. Some of them aren't moving, so either they blacked out from the pain, or she killed them.

That won't earn her any favors with the Maker.

Fuck it, I'm not going to sit around and watch her be cornered and attacked for a moment longer, especially if it condemns her more thoroughly to hells below. I don't care if she hates my guts, I refuse to sit around and watch her fight alone.

I flare my wings and leap off the roof just as I spot a large boulder pitching forward from a window below me, right above her head.

That's the real threat. Even Scarla can't defend herself against being crushed to death.

I won't make it in time. All I can do is bellow, and she glances up. Her eyes widen, and she darts out of the way just as the giant boulder slams into the ground, ripping up a few more cobblestones.

I land heavily on the ground beside her, scanning her frantically for injuries.

Pain hits me like a falling mountain, agony so intense I can't think, and my glamor falls from my face as I stumble to my knees.

Instantly, the pain stops, and Scarla is kneeling beside me. "Zaden? I thought I recognized your color magic, but your face...are you okay?"

The tenderness in her voice has me on cloud nine. I could lick her concern and sweetness right out of the air.

I unkink and straighten up, kneeling beside her, our chests mere inches apart. "Hello, Scarla."

Time stretches, as vast as the emotional gulf between us.

She's even more beautiful up close. Those startling brown eyes, the curve of her jaw, and that wild copper hair.

Her face is open, vulnerable, more vulnerable than I've seen it in months. "You came," she says simply.

I nod. I take her hands in mine. They're small but strong and contain a world of power. "I don't care if we only have a few years together, if I end up in heaven and you in hell. Let's just enjoy the time we have. The brevity will make the years even sweeter."

She squeezes my hands. "I agree."

A laugh bubbles up from within me. "You agree? That is so unlike you. Usually you're the first to contradict anything I say."

She grins, and it lights up her face. I've missed her smile so much. This one is looser and freer than any I've seen on her, and it lifts me to the stars.

She pushes my shoulder playfully. "It's hard to agree with

you when you're so often wrong. But this time, we both happen to be right."

I can't wait a moment longer. I snake an arm around her back and pull her flush against me, then press my lips against the sweetest, sexiest mouth in the world.

Scarla

Pressed against Zaden's body, wrapped in his arms, the monster in my chest is finally quiet.

I mumble into his shoulder. "That boulder would have killed me if you hadn't been here."

He squeezes me tighter. "I missed you, mortal."

I missed him too, like a fucking organ. But I can't have him getting all arrogant, so I mumble again, "Oh, really? I didn't realize you were gone." But I burrow deeper into his black-clad shoulder, exposing my words as lies.

He pulls me tight one last time, his wild lilies of the forest scent mixed with tangy fear. He finds his feet. He's wearing black pants with lots of pockets and a fitted black shirt, and I've never seen anything hotter.

His chiseled face is hard, with a three-day growth and skin tanned a light gold. His lips are full, soft, kissable, and his broad forehead is furrowed in concern. "There will be more angels around. We have to get you out of here."

He could say *I told you so*, and he'd be bloody right. He told me the Cloaked King always kept his identity secret so he wouldn't be hunted by the other angels. I detest them all for their arrogance, but I showed interplanetary levels of arrogance myself by just shouting my existence to the world.

Now I'm reaping the rewards.

Zaden pulls me to my feet. I deliberately land close against his sculpted chest, bouncing off his hard muscles.

I can't keep my eyes off his corded arms while he casts a net of purple-white magic over my face, sparking a light tingle on my skin. He does the same to himself, and his features change, rearranging; his black hair lightens, and his jaw softens.

I gasp. I'm not ready to lose sight of my gorgeous angel. How did I ever go a whole month without him?

It takes me a moment to figure out what happened, then I clap my hands and wink. "Is this a glamor? What do I look like? Glamorous?"

Zaden rolls his eyes at me, sweeps up my hand in his huge one, and then tugs me out to the main street.

The streets are busy, and I follow Zaden's lead. "Where are we going?" I hiss.

"Oh, I know a place." He smirks as he says it, and a pulse of desire spins through me.

I lean in and squeeze the corded muscles of his upper arm. They're his muscles, the ones I know so well. Only our faces are glamored, so his body is all Zaden.

His muscles tense under my touch, and his hand grips mine tighter. I run my fingers up and down, marking the contours and firmness and remembering just how sexy he is.

"Do you see any angels?"

"Nope. No glowing people, just a bunch of colorfully dressed towns folk."

I switch the hand he's holding to my other one, so I can explore his body better. My hand wanders higher, up over his shoulder and across his back. Every muscled groove is a sensual toxin invading my body.

"You're killing me here, mortal," he growls.

"What?" I ask innocently.

"I can smell your desire, and it's driving me crazy."

I look down and see a massive erection tenting his trousers. I snake my hand down.

Still no angels in sight, and we're still walking the broad paving stones of one of the nicer parts of Desert's Maw, and I still have no idea of our destination. But now, I don't care.

I drag a hand around the top of his low-slung pants, his hip, and the front. I ease the front of his pants forward so his cock can spring up, so huge it juts out the top of his waistband.

I close my hand around the tip, and he groans.

My panties are so wet I wonder that all the townsfolk passing us can't smell me, and the sound of my angel's arousal makes me even wetter.

He sounds so good. And his cock in my hand feels like heaven. Warm, hard, pulsing. Only the tip pokes through onto my bare skin, and I caress it, circling it slowly with my thumb.

My angel groans again, and my breasts tighten, my nipples peaking the front of my shirt.

It is delicious torture, wanting him so badly but being on a public street.

"In here," he growls. He yanks me roughly off the street into an inn and throws a bunch of coins to the surprised innkeeper, who points us toward a bedroom.

We stumble up the stairs, me first. Zaden runs his hands all over, from my waist, over the swell of my hips, and down my legs as we climb, and it feels so good.

He kicks the bedroom door closed behind him then cages me against it with his arms. "Tell me you missed me, mortal," he growls.

I want to deny him, to be coquettish and flirty, but I'm breathy and panting. "I missed you."

"Tell me you love me."

I pause, and he smashes his lips against mine, hungry and burning for me like I burn for him.

I devour him, lost in his mouth, the sensations of his lips and tongue, the biting, the sucking, the owning.

With my back pressed against the wooden door and his lips pressed against mine, I yearn for his touch. Everywhere.

My breasts are full and heavy, desperate for his hands, his tongue, his attention.

His hands are on my dark green shirt, unbuttoning slowly, exposing more of my alabaster flesh.

He undoes the button right between my nipples and groans again, then ducks his head and kisses the swell of my breasts.

I throw my head back in ecstasy, not caring, hitting it against the wooden door, but I don't care.

His deft fingers keep working until my shirt is undone, then he slips it off my shoulders, kissing me as I thrust my chest forward.

He pulls down my bra cups so my breasts sit up and forward, and he growls at them greedily. He takes one in his mouth and cups the other gently with a hand, squeezing the nipple between two fingers.

I throw back my head, engulfed in ecstasy, but I need to look again.

His dark head, tongue dancing over my feverish skin, and huge hand on my breasts are the best things I've ever seen. The wetness between my thighs is growing unbearable, an ache that needs attention.

He kisses my belly and unbuttons my pants. I wriggle out

of them, and he strips down my dark green panties, breathing heavily as they clear the swell of my hips and fall in a puddle at my feet.

"So fucking perfect," he murmurs, then he pins me against the door, one shoulder pressed into my belly so my back is flattened against the wood and my pelvis tilted up. He grabs my leg and throws it over his other shoulder, but I'm pinned so firmly in place that I'm in no danger of losing my balance.

"That's more like it," he growls, staring at my exposed pussy and salivating.

I push his head down, gripping his hair hard so he can't get away, and he dives down and feasts on me. He licks me slowly, long, luscious licks that have me quivering and my legs trembling. Then he circles my clit with his tongue, pressing hard, and I cry out.

I throw back my head, but I can't keep away for long; the sight of his head feasting on my pussy is too delicious.

He concentrates his tongue on my clit and slips two fingers inside me, curling them slightly to hit my magical spot. The pleasure is unbearable, every bit as mind-altering as the pain pits. The world is narrowed onto my angel and my building orgasm.

It swells and builds, and my legs lose strength entirely. I sag against his shoulder as his expert tongue brings me to climax, and I shudder, screaming out his name as I fall to pieces around him.

He keeps licking until my long climax is complete, then he gently eases his shoulder from my belly and catches me when I fall.

His eyes are hooded and hungry. He carries me to the bed, lays me on the edge, and kneels beside me. His tip is eager and hot, and he slides into me easily despite his length because I am dripping in desire.

He thrusts into me firmly, and my breasts bounce, drawing his gaze and making him moan.

He is so handsome, and his green eyes have turned coal black in his ravenous lust.

The flame of desire in my body that he just doused sparks to life, and I wrap my legs around his waist, pulling him in closer with every thrust.

He unglamors his wings, and they flare out behind him, their black tips brushing the ceiling.

The effect on me is instantaneous, and the spark of desire inside me becomes a raging inferno.

A single angel feather can make a room full of mortals come, and I am within arms' reach of hundreds.

I sit up, my breasts jiggling against his chest, drawing another moan of pleasure from his perfect lips. I brush a finger down his wing, feeling those soft midnight feathers under my hot fingers.

The contact heightens both our pleasure. Zaden shivers as I stroke his feathers, and he increases the pace of his thrusts. The fire between my thighs burns harder and hotter, and with one final stroke, my muscles clench around Zaden's cock, pulling out his orgasm with my own.

I clutch his shoulders as I wilt, and our movements slow. He eases out of me, and I wait for the wicked gleam in his eyes, the flirty banter. He picks me up, tosses me onto the mattress, then rolls beside me, staring at me intensely.

"Cat got your tongue, angel?" I tease.

It's fascinating to watch the black disperse from his pupils, leaving them their usual intense green.

He doesn't smile, just stares at me with a wild intensity I can't interpret.

Finally, he rests back on the pillow and pulls me close so my head rests on his chest.

"Go to sleep, mortal."

Zaden

That was the best night's sleep I've ever had. Even better to wake and find my naked little mortal curled up beside me, her head resting on my chest. Even the saliva dripping from her open mouth is adorable.

She senses me waking. "Morning, angel."

"Morning, mortal."

She smiles sleepily. "Why doesn't that nickname bother me anymore?"

I run a hand over her shoulder and down her arm all the way to her hip. The X-shaped scar on her hip, carved into her flesh by Xerxes, reminds me that I did the right thing by killing him, even if it earned me a thousand hunting demons.

I smile. "Because you've realized how amazing I am, and everything I do is excellent."

She shoves me playfully then elbows me in the ribs. "No, that definitely can't be it. You've just worn me down, I suppose." Her smile is delicious, and I want to plant a kiss on every one of her freckles.

"Besides, I'm the Queen around here. You should bow down to me, not the other way around."

"I will never bow down to you, mortal."

She brushes a finger against my lips. "Oh, you will. One day."

I'm already hard. I will probably spend every moment of this mortal's life as hard as steel.

"Have you been experimenting with Inflict over this past month?" I run my hands up and down her back, feeling her delicious soft skin and marveling at her fragility. She might be strong for a human, but she's crushable for an angel. It makes her more precious.

She tilts her head. "Of course I have. Why?"

My cock twitches in anticipation of what I'm about to say. "Can you inflict pleasure on yourself?"

I smell the nectar that forms between her legs, and she bites her lower lip seductively. "Ye-es."

"Show me."

She smiles wickedly then settles back against her pillow, pulling the sheet over her body.

"No. I want to see every inch of you. Stand up and show me how you pleasure yourself."

She assesses me for a moment, her eyes narrowing, and I hope to Hades she agrees to this. Nothing could be sexier than seeing my woman naked and writhing in pleasure.

"Fine. But I'm not sharing my Inflict with you," she teases.

"Trust me, I won't need it," I growl. I'm already hard enough to burst just from his conversation and her closeness.

She slides to her feet gracefully, and I perch on the bed's foot to see every bit of her.

She's glorious. Smooth alabaster skin, large breasts that bounce with her every slightest movement, generous hips that sway and move as though she were created just for me.

Her legs are long and lean, tapering and curving in all the right ways. Even her bare white feet are fucking perfect.

She moves toward me and bends over, and her breasts fill my

view. I think she will touch me, and I don't think I'll be able to stop her if she does because my willpower is teetering on the edge. But she just rips the sheet off my lap, scowling. "I have to be able to see you too," she insists.

My cock springs free. I get the eerie sense that my body belongs to her now as my skin tingles under her command.

She smiles silkily, then stands up, and her breasts and hips jiggle and sway into place.

"Now," I growl. I need to maintain some power in this situation.

I can't see magic the way she can, but I can sure as hells below see its effect. She throws her head back, her copper hair wild and tousled around her neck and shoulders, her back arched toward me. She clamps both hands over her breasts and catches her nipples between two fingers, and a small moan escapes her lips.

She is skin and flesh and heat and lust, a walking dream. Her salted berry arousal fills the room, so thick I can almost taste its sweetness on my tongue.

I murmur an obscenity, watching as she pleasures herself, writhing and dancing before me, all sinuous curves and heated desire.

She slowly moves one hand down her belly, over the curve of her hip, and I imagine it as my own hand, tracing her ins and outs, her mountains and valleys, feeling her beneath my rough palms.

Then her hand is between her thighs, and she moans again, arching her back and thrusting her breasts forward. Her nipples are peaked, yearning and reaching for me, the way my cock yearns for her.

I'm touching myself now in long firm strokes, but my eyes

never leave her body.

The hand between her thighs moves rhythmically, and she rocks into it. She's fucking mesmerizing. Her moans grow louder and higher, and I move my hand up and down my cock in the same rhythm as Scarla's hand, imagining we are joined and that her motion is my motion.

This female is everything.

The sound of her peaking in ecstasy is my undoing, and I shoot hot cum across the room, spilling some on her feet.

She's panting, I'm panting, and we lock eyes. A strand of copper hair is in her mouth, highlighting her lips, her fragile beauty, and I know I've made the right decision.

I cross the room in an instant, holding her against my skin. She's hot and slightly damp from sweat. I lick the salt from her forehead and plant a kiss there. "Impressive," I murmur, and she laughs into my chest.

Scarla is sexy as she dresses, and I watch every movement. When she bends over to put her legs in her pants, I can't help smacking her round ass. "That's for leaving me for a month," I tease.

She shimmies into her pants. "You deserved it."

It's dangerous territory, but I can't help going there. This woman makes me want to talk. "For putting your life ahead of a maid's? Ahead of everyone else's?"

Her lips thin. "For treating me like a child and taking away my choices. Never do that again."

Power radiates from her. I don't need Gaze to see just how powerful Scarla is. "I won't. I promise."

"Good boy."

I watch as she buttons her dark green shirt, hiding those lovely breasts. "Not a boy. What are our plans today? A spot of sightseeing and a long lunch?"

She smiles wistfully. "That would be nice. But you know as well as I do that we have work to do. We need to find the Ring of Roth that your bitch ex-girlfriend stole so you can return to heaven, and—"

"That suddenly seems less important. I'd rather just hang out with you."

She bristles. "Well, I wouldn't. I want to go to my grave knowing you have secured your return ticket to heaven. Otherwise, I'll come and haunt you for eternity."

I smile sinfully. "That sounds delightful. I could definitely get on board with the haunting."

She cocks out a hip. "No, you couldn't. I would stand before you ass-naked every day, and you wouldn't be able to touch me."

I shiver dramatically. "Fine. We'll get the Ring of Roth. But we also need to do your thing."

She scans the room for personal belongings, then heads to the door. "My thing? Are you referring to my noble search for justice and ensuring that the people who have it all learn how to share?"

I nod. "That's the one. The truth is, it's kind of my thing now too."

She pauses with her hand on the doorknob. "It is?"

"Yep. I came here via the Undercity, looking for you, and I noticed how poor everybody was. I'd never really noticed before if you can believe that."

"An arrogant angel like you? Trust me, I can believe it."

I shrug. "Anyway, I think they deserve a little more."

She studies me for a long moment, assessing my sincerity, then flings herself across the room and into my arms, smelling

44

delightfully musky. "Did I mention how much I love you?"

I kiss her. "You don't mention it nearly enough."

She breaks away and goes back to the door. "You came via the Undercity?"

"Yes. I didn't think you'd be able to get across the desert. How did you get here?"

She opens the door, and an angel falls through it. He'd been sitting with his back against the door, and now he's lying half in the room, looking as confused and outraged as I feel. Unkempt white-blond curls escape a loose braid, and he thuds loudly on the floor.

"What the fuck?" he asks, getting to his feet. "Give a guy some notice next time you interrupt his sleep."

Adrenaline floods my body, and I am instantly on high alert. With one movement, I shove Scarla behind me and pull Ashmodu from its scabbard. "You have to get through me, Lazius, if you want to get to Scarla."

A single unruly tuft of gold-streaked hair hangs down his face, untamed and wild. His locks are a tangled mess, pulled back into a rough braid. His clothing is dirt-stained and disheveled, and his skin is ashen. The sour smell of alcohol wafts from him like a heavy fog. I recognize him from Cloaked Council, but I only know that he lives somewhere in the far south of Aubia and keeps to himself.

Scarla laughs. "What in hells below are you doing here, Lazius? How did you find me?"

Some of the tension bleeds from me, but I keep my sword in my hand. "Do you know this angel?"

Scarla comes to my side and presses a gentle hand on my sword arm, making me lower it. "Yes, he's the answer to your question. He flew me here from Solren."

The Maker-be-damned angel looks smug, and I want to slap him for it—helping Scarla is my job, not his. But he kept her safe, so I let it go.

Scarla's hands are on her hips. "How did you find us, Lazius?"

The angel sniffs dramatically toward our crotches. "I could smell you guys from The Jagged Tooth." He sniffs some more. "Plus, Mahari had you followed and told me you were here."

"Why?" I glower.

Scarla brushes past us both, heading outside. "You can tell us on the way. We're headed to The Jagged Tooth to find out where Mahari's resistance is headquartered. The bar is the only lead we have."

The angel stage whispers, "Keep your voice down, gigantor." He trots after her down the stairs and into the dawn streets, which teem with people.

Gigantor? I'll get to the bottom of that later.

"We don't need to go to The Jagged Tooth to ask where the headquarters are," Lazius says. "Mahari already told me. Follow me." He takes the lead, and I fall in beside, Scarla.

"Why didn't you kill us last night?" I demand.

Lazius throws up his hands. "Why is everyone so obsessed with me not-killing them? I actually prefer not-killing people if I can help it."

"Aren't you allied with the other angels?" Scarla asks.

"No way. The best thing you ever did was kill that slimeball, Belial. Who would've thought that slimy loser was the Cloaked King? Good riddance to him. Even with your twitchy pain finger, you're a million times better than him."

Twitchy pain finger? I'll ask Scarla about that later. My list of questions is growing fast.

"Why do you hate Belial so much? What did he do to you?"

Scarla asks. One of my favorite things about Scarla is that she doesn't do idle chitchat. If she says something, it's important, so I suspect her intuition here is spot on. The Cloaked King must have done something terrible to Lazius.

The angel's stride falters, and we catch up with him. He sighs. "The Cloaked King imprisoned me under his castle for a hundred years. He used Inflict to keep me there. I could barely think, let alone fight or plan an escape." His jocular tone has disappeared, and his voice is flat and quiet. "He let me out once a year to visit my home so I could remember what I'd lost. That kept the pain of separation fresh in my mind."

Scarla's soft tone matches his. "Separation from who?"

"A mortal I fell in love with." He hooks a thumb at me. "This guy is not the only one who can fall in love with a human woman. And after she died, the Cloaked King let me go."

"Bastard," Scarla murmurs.

There has to be more to the story. Belial was a filthy power-hungry creep, but he'd never gone that far with any other angel. "Why you?"

Lazius shakes off his pain like a dog shaking water. "Because I'm so powerful he thought I'd take over his reign." He grins mischievously, implying it's a joke, but I wonder if it really is.

Maybe there's more to Lazius than I thought.

Scarla

Lazius leads us straight back to The Jagged Tooth. The rusty sign of the incisor squeaks back and forth under a gentle dawn breeze.

I look up at him. "I thought you said we didn't need to return here?"

He grins. "I said we didn't need to come back here to find out where the headquarters are. That's because the headquarters are here."

Zadan groans.

I pat Lazius on the back. "Lead the way."

The door dude takes one look at me and lets us pass without comment, setting a self-satisfied glow inside me. It's good having power.

It's dawn, so the overnight patrons are heading out, and the daytime revelers are filing in.

The interior is familiar to me now, the bar running down the middle of the room, separating the smoke-filled tavern from the moan-filled pits for pleasure and pain. It is dim and depressing after the brisk walk in the fresh air.

"This way." Lazius leads us through the bumping and jostling crowd, around the pits of pleasure and pain, and back to a small doorway beside the woman with Inflict, who sits patiently on her chair.

She ignored me last time, so I can't help offering a little jab of pleasure at her as we pass. Her eyes immediately flow to Zaden, scanning his muscular body and square jaw, and I regret having filled her with lust. I grab Zaden's arm possessively and hurry him past her.

Through the doorway is a back room with shelving filled with liquor bottles and beer kegs. Lazius rubs his hands together. "Now we're talking."

"Don't tell me you brought us here just so you could get drunk," Zaden says with a snarl.

Lazius isn't fazed by the show of anger. "Nope, the drunk part is just a perk."

A wooden trapdoor is smack bang in the room's center, and I pull it open, wincing under the loud creak of the hinge. "I'm guessing we go down here?"

This building is laid out like the Lowtown huts in Malanox. A portion of the building is above ground, but every home has a dugout underneath to provide shelter from the extreme temperatures.

We climb down the ladder into a standard living space, just like the ones in Lowtown. Well, like the only one I've been inside, anyway. I used to check in on Leesa's friend, Raylee, and this room is a carbon copy of hers. A narrow chimney to let smoke out and let light in, a snowmelt catch for water, a bench for cooking, a table and a couple of chairs, and a sleeping pallet pushed into a corner.

"Impressive," Zaden deadpans.

One thing is different. A bookshelf filled with books looks out of place. Usually books are reserved for the rich, and nothing else in this room screams wealth.

"Give me a hand." I lean a shoulder into the bookshelf and push, and when the angels help me, it slides smoothly across the stone floor, revealing another trapdoor and ladder down.

Lazius nods smugly. "I'm not just a drunken blabbermouth, you know. That's just to cover up my true self. Like a glamor, you know?"

I pat his arm. "Well, it's a very good one. You come across exactly like a drunken blabbermouth."

Lazius smiles. "Thank you."

I grin and climb down the ladder, followed by the two angels. I'm greeted by a blade to my throat, so I still. Somebody switches off the lights to disadvantage us newcomers, but I can see clearly with my Gaze-glowing angels. I pinpoint the three women holding blades to our throats and douse them with pain so they fall to the ground. "Turn the lights on, please. My friends here can't see in the dark." I indicate the hulking angels beside me.

Zaden hums in pleasure at my comment, loving my power almost as much as I do.

When no light appears, I randomly pick another person to stab with pain. He doubles over with a loud groan. The beauty of this approach is that none of them will be permanently injured or even damaged at all, and I get to flex my skills.

"I can take you down individually, or you can just light a candle. Your choice."

A few dozen figures lurk in the dim light, and finally, one sparks a flame.

"Thank you, that's better," I say.

The space is larger than the upstairs, like a community space.

"Where's the bar?" Lazius asks, narrowing his eyes. "Don't tell me I have to go back upstairs."

One of the figures on the floor stammers, "D-downstairs. The kitchen is downstairs, and the bedrooms are below that."

Lazius whistles. I'm impressed too. I can imagine the hours they spent digging to make this place so many levels deep.

I clear my throat. "We're looking for Mahari."

A tall black woman with a half-shaved head and a warrior's stare enters the light. "You're looking better," she says. She is statuesque and imposing, a woman who gives away nothing.

Zaden shifts his weight. This must be hard for him, coming face-to-face with a group of mortals who hate angels so much they want to rid them from the earth.

I take a deep breath. "We are here to tell you that the time has come to rise against our oppressors."

A man from the dark calls out, almost a shriek. "Are those angels? They look like angels. No human is that good-looking. She brought angels here."

I stab the man with pain to shut him up, but it's too late. Murmurs ripple through the room, accompanied by the schlick of blades being drawn.

I hold out my hands. "I am here to tell you the time for our uprising has arrived. These angels are on our side." We haven't actually run Lazius through the entire plan, so I just pray to the Maker that he doesn't contradict me. I'll convince him to get fully on board later. "These two powerful angels will fight beside us for justice. And you have me."

A couple of women scoff, and I whirl on them. "Pleasure or pain, ladies?" They don't bother to answer. "Pleasure, I presume?" I drill them with lust, and their expressions turn hungry and hooded, and they run their hands down their bodies.

I release them before things get embarrassing because I'm here to win allies, not enemies. "I have the dyad of Gaze and

Inflict, and—"

"Prove it."

Several vestiges are dotted among the crowd, their colored glows dim compared to the angels. I stab a finger at each of them in turn. "Grower." The green one. "Healer." The bright, sunny yellow. "Clout." The vibrant blyberry strongman. "Keen." The hot pink of fevered flesh. Impressed murmurs follow my words.

"The Cloaked King of the Angels is dead. Our counterparts across the desert are prepared. Now is the time to strike."

The crowd's mood shifts into excitement and readiness, with folks talking over the top of each other, planning and predicting.

One voice rises above the rest. "Can you kill the angels, once and for all?"

I twist my lips. "Only a celestial blade can kill an angel. But our task is not to murder them, but to launch a coup and install somebody who would rule with humans instead of over them."

The natural person for the job is me, but it's the last thing I want to do. I push aside the knowledge that I am the only being who holds the dyad and focus on how my words are rippling through the room.

They start another round of murmuring and guessing, but in the end, it doesn't matter if they agree with the plan to keep most angels alive. We have no way to kill dozens of angels, and now that I've befriended two, I have no desire to either.

All I need are their bodies and their support.

Zaden's voice booms across the crowd. "Can we count on your aid?"

The crowd mutters again, and Mahari steps forward. "We will discuss this among ourselves. Return at the morrow's dawn, and we will have our answer."

Our coup won't succeed without their help. Almost a thousand warriors will make the difference between success and failure, but there is little more I can do. I must wait for their reply.

It's going to be a long twenty-four hours.

Zaden

The following day, Scarla and I leave our hotel for The Jagged Tooth at early dawn.

Lazius didn't answer our knock at his door, so we left without him.

I sweep up Scarla's hand in mine. "Do you think Lazius slept under the bar last night?"

She grins. "He probably slept in the pleasure pit. That place will be splattered with angel cum."

I give a warning growl. "Don't think about that male's cum."

She lifts a shoulder. "Or what?"

I lean down and kiss her shoulder. "Or I'll plunge Ashmodu through his weaselly little heart, and you can watch him bleed out on the stained carpet."

She shakes her head. "So aggressive. I kinda love it."

We're quite the pair. An avenging angel and a master tormentor.

Two men wearing bright yellow robes, each with a baby on his hip, almost bump into us as they rush past in the opposite direction. "I remember thinking how colorfully dressed people were the first time I was here," Scarla says.

"Mmm, I've been thinking about that too."

"Really?" She perks up at that news. "The colorful fashion?"

I snort. "No. About your first visit here. Right after you discovered your mom was still alive." We walk in silence for a few beats, our footsteps light on the wide pavings stones. "Do you want to go see her again?"

Scarla bristles. "No."

"Are you sure? I know she disappointed you, but—"

Scarla scoffs. "Now, there's an understatement. I thought she was changing the world, and she was just a fucking circus clown."

I squeeze her hand. She's been disappointed by her mom time and again, I understand that. "Are you sure? It might make you feel...better. Are you still angry at her?"

Scarla chews her lip. "I'm not mad at her anymore, not really. But I can't forgive her for abandoning me when I was just a little girl and running off just to act a fool for money. Why would she do that?"

Scarla's gaze is locked on the broad paving stones at our feet, but I can see her trembling with emotion. I cannot think of any reason Scarla's mom would abandon her. Why anyone would ever leave this person. "I can't excuse what she did, but maybe you'd feel better if you saw her again."

Scarla's jaw clench. "Not now. Maybe later. Like, years later."

Whatever Scarla chooses to do, I will support her. No matter what. I learned the lesson of going behind her back and doing what I thought was best, and I almost lost her. She's right—she's a grown-ass woman who can make her own decisions. My job is just to support her.

It's late dawn by the time we push past the doorman at The Jagged Tooth. Lazius is leaning against the bar, talking loudly to the poor barman, not intimidated by the eyeball tattooed onto the man's sewn-shut eyelid.

Scarla raises her voice so I can hear her above the daytime crowd just settling into their pleasure and pain pits and settling into their drinks. "I didn't know angels could even get drunk," she says, spotting Lazius at the bar with his long pale fingers clasped around a frothy green drink.

"No need to shout, mortal. I have celestial hearing," I say.

She shoves me. "Show off."

I grin. "Angels can get drunk, but we sober up quickly. If we want to stay drunk, we need to keep drinking."

Lazius obviously hears that remark because he spins on his barstool and raises a glass. "Cheers to hard work!" His white-blond hair has been freshly braided and looks neat for a change.

We convince him to put down his drink and follow us. Around the pits and through the doorway, down the public ladder, then the private one to the hidden lounge area.

No blades pierce our flesh today, and the light stays on. The crowd is quiet, but the mood is simmering.

Scarla wastes no time. She pitches her voice loud. "Will you join our cause?"

Our mission is to ensure the other angels acknowledge Scarla as their Queen so she can do better in this world. Better for the angels who aren't in power and better for the mortals.

I don't voice that thought because the talking is best left to the mortal. And she's doing a good job, commanding every ear in the room.

Mahari's voice rings clear, almost matching Scarla's. "We have debated through the night. We will join you."

Scarla beams beside me, radiating joy.

I'm happy too, but I'm also worried. Scarla will hurtle head-strong into anything, and keeping her safe in the upcoming battle will be hard. Humans do not fare well in arguments with angels.

I want a changed world, and I want her to achieve her goals—otherwise, she will never be truly happy.

But mostly, I want her safe. I want her alive.

So my joy at the Desert's Maw resistance agreeing to join our cause is neutered by fear for Scarla.

Talk turns to logistics. Mahari has nearly a thousand warriors, and each one must cross the Dead Desert. Lazius and I cannot hope to fly them all over; that would take weeks or months.

"We must use the Nashanti," Mahari says. The Nashanti is a desert tribe, the only people who can survive in that harsh environment. "They can guide us across."

"We will walk with you," Lazius says, drawing every eye. That was unexpected. Why would we walk when we can fly?

Lazius turns to us and shrugs. "A leader never asks for his subjects to give more than he is willing to give himself."

Hmm. I really was wrong about that angel—he is more than just a drunken blabbermouth.

The other drunken blabbermouth, the Oracle of Howlka, tole me to cross the hottest desert in my search for the Ring of Roth. So when Scarla agrees to cross the desert on foot, I don't voice any objections.

But the Dead Desert is a harsh place and the ultimate equalizer. It kills without discrimination.

Scarla

The bench is warm under my legs, still radiating the heat it absorbed during the day. I arrived just before dusk, marveling at the bench's existence.

Nothing like this exists at home in Malanox. There, dusk and dawn are so short that everybody is always running to get their errands done before they need to return indoors. Here, with their extended dawn and dusk, there is a bench just for sitting on. Outside.

At early dusk, the hardiest Desert Mawkers wander outside, going about their business. There is more freedom and joy here, I think. Probably because of the weather. Or the lack of angel overlords.

Two young girls scamper from a building behind me and join a line of children chanting a song about school. I stop a passing woman to ask what the children are doing.

"Why, they're going to school, of course. It's the walking train, and they sing to let families know when they are passing."

I can see why Mom likes it here. So much color, so much joy.

I'm on my feet, following the chain of singsong children, but I keep walking when they duck into a tunnel beneath a sign reading Marigold District Schoolhouse.

I have a lot to think over. Plans are underway for our move

to Solren. That will be like a train too, but through the harsh desert and without any singing. We leave tomorrow at dawn sharp.

I needed to get away, so I excused myself from the preparations. Zaden glamored me so I could safely show my face outside, but he warned it would fade if I went too far from him.

So why in hells below am I walking away?

I need to think. Everything is going so fast now. Mahari has committed hundreds of warriors to fight our cause, and now doubts are settling into my bones.

We want to overthrow the angels and put someone better in charge. Everybody assumes it will be me because I have the dyad of Gaze and Inflict.

But what if I'm no better than the last Cloaked King? I've already proved to be a moody bitch, and, as Lazius keeps pointing out, I have an itchy torture finger. I tortured him for hours, and he's on my side. What will I do to my enemies?

It used to be so easy. When I was a little girl, I was full of noble goals, like making the world a better place. But it's hard to keep those noble goals in mind when power thrums through my body and betrayals burn in my memories.

All I want is to hurt people, to seek my revenge.

So what if I end up just as bad as Belial? If one month with the dyad turned me into a torture-hungry maniac, what will one year do? Or a decade? Or an entire lifetime?

As I wander further from The Jagged Tooth, where Zaden is, my face begins to tingle. The glamor is fading.

I should turn around and scurry back to Zaden, but I never was very good at scurrying.

Besides, I've reached my destination.

Layered strips of red and blue ox hide form a circular tent

called a big top. It radiates warmth and vibrancy, and its colorful beauty takes my breath away.

Zaden asked whether I wanted to meet with my mom, and I said no. I don't know if I was telling the truth or lying, but somehow my feet have brought me here, where she works. Where she demonstrates her vestigial powers for money. I'd rather be paid for carnal pleasure, like that woman I saw the other day in Solren.

The tingling over my face intensifies, and a noise behind me makes me jump. Incense from the circus tent drugs the air, and I sneeze.

I stare at the entrance doorway. Mom is inside there, the famous Resplendent Rose. I could take a few steps and see her again, the woman I spent my whole life wishing to be with. But now that I can, I don't want to anymore.

Last time I was here, I was filled with anger, and everything she told me stoked my fury.

I sigh and turn away. I've had enough of rage. I just want to be by Zaden's side, fighting for a good cause.

I head toward the hotel where we're staying. The darkness is almost complete. A few stragglers sprint along, desperately trying to get someplace before the freeze.

It's just the angels and me on the streets now. Without my glamor I am exposed, and without Zaden I feel vulnerable. I quicken my pace, sticking to the edges of the roads where my form might be lost among the buildings.

I whirl around at a footstep behind me, my heart rattling. My one-hundred-percent certainty of my own infallibility has evaporated. Almost being crushed to death by a falling stone will do that.

No bright glowing figures are in the darkness, so no angels.

Either that, or they're getting better at hiding.

"Get it together, Scarla," I mutter.

I resume walking, but at a tap on my shoulder, I spin and shoot pain at my attacker. She doubles over and shrieks, her fiery auburn hair obscuring her face.

"Mom? Is that you?"

As soon as I withdraw the pain, she straightens up, her eyes wide. "Scarla! It really is you. I saw you standing outside the big top, so I followed you. I don't know if you can believe this...But I really am glad to see you."

I can't get used to her accent. She no longer speaks with the gentle lilting tone of the South but with a mixed accent peppered with the harsh guttural syllables of the North. It makes her sound unreal like she's still performing.

I breathe deeply, searching within myself for anger. "I believe you."

She blinks at me, hopefully. "Really?"

"It doesn't mean I forgive you. You left Leesa and me when we were just kids, and you left Dad to raise us alone. I don't know if I can ever forgive you for that. As far as I'm concerned, your one job was to be my mom, and you fucked up."

To her credit, she doesn't back away from my condemnation. She holds my gaze. "I never was very good at being a mother. I'm too selfish for that. I'm sorry I couldn't be better."

That's it. That's the truth of our relationship, and there's no avoiding it. I wanted a mom, but she couldn't be a mom. Maybe there's nothing to forgive. She's done the only thing she could do, been the only person she could be, lived the only life she could live. And I've done the same.

Doesn't mean I'll let her off easy. "I could never understand the choice you made. You can choose not to be selfish. You can choose to put aside your own dreams to meet your responsibilities. When you had a family with Dad, you took on a shitload of responsibility and just threw it away."

She nods, and the tears in her eyes seem genuine. "I know. I don't expect you to understand. I just wanted to come and say hello."

The truth is, part of me does understand. Life in Desert's Maw is easier than in Malanox. More vibrant, full of the color I've yearned for my entire life. I used to dye my shirts blue with blyberries just to escape the visual monotony of the Undercity.

I nod. "Okay...Hello."

She smiles, and it brings her face to life. She's happy here, so at least that's something.

She pulls me into a hug. Her body's slim but strong. "Tell your father... Tell him I wish I could have been a better wife. Tell him I wish I could have been better at loving him."

I pull away from the hug, patting down the yellow shirt I borrowed from Mahari. "Tell him yourself."

Mom smiles sadly, and I know she will never return to Malanox, not even to see her husband. The spark of anger rekindles in my chest, my monster coming to life.

I back away. "Well, I have to go."

"It was nice seeing you, berry," she says, and I don't correct her use of my nickname. Only Dad calls me that, but Mom used to, so I'll allow it this one time.

I turn and walk along the street, right at snowfall, and thick flakes plummet to the ground around me. I feel lighter, and the monster in my chest goes back to sleep.

Scarla

Mahari has an extensive network of sympathizers throughout Desert's Maw, all willing to risk and sacrifice to improve their lives. Not only warriors and fighters but also cooks, clothesmakers, bakers, and chicken farmers.

She rallied them overnight to gather as many resources as possible to help her crew across the desert.

A dozen houses on the edge of the Dead Desert were used as inns, the warriors crammed in overnight so they'd be ready to run in the morning at dawn sharp.

Our Nashanti guide, a brown-skinned man with black eyes and a shaved head named Saheel rejected some of the warriors last night, refusing to guide them across the desert. Only the fittest and fastest will make it.

We will have to scurry between hiding places, sprinting across the desert during dawn and dusk, and if we don't make it to the next underground hidey-hole, we die.

The further south we travel, the shorter dawn and dusk will become, and the less time we'll have available to travel.

So our numbers have reduced, but hundreds of Desert's Maw fighters are still waiting and jostling, ready to run across the desert.

Zaden and I arrive pre-dawn, standing knee-deep in the snow

that fell overnight. I'm wearing my washed green shirt and black pants, and Zaden is in his usual armor of black pants with a bunch of pockets and a black shirt that hugs his muscles. It's like he wants me to be too distracted to run.

When the first ray of sun hits the horizon, Saheel lets out a great roar and begins sprinting across the open desert, running faster than I thought possible through the deep snow.

Men and women spill from the houses around us and run after him, their thundering feet like a stampede of thermo-oxen.

Zaden and I let them pass and then follow behind. Lazius does the same. As the only three who will survive full sun, we should bring up the rear.

The going is tough. After a few minutes, the snow begins melting, turning into slush, but at least I don't have to pick up my feet as high to push through it.

I fall behind the other runners, just on the heels of another couple of stragglers. Panic etches the face of a young woman in bright purple pants, making this all seem very real.

She's falling behind the others and will die if she loses any more ground. It's not something I've had to deal with in living memory because I've had my temperature resistance since I was tiny. Of course, the rhythms of my days have always centered around the sun's movements, but the panic on this woman's face hits home. I yell out some encouragement.

Zaden sticks to my side, a comforting presence. Even though I know I'll be okay, some fear has wormed into my heart, and having him beside me keeps it at bay.

The snow melts completely, and my socks are soaked through even in my thick ox-hide boots. My muscles are burning, and my lungs ache, but I am lagging further and further behind the main pack.

The sun is almost entirely risen, just the tiniest smidge short of a perfect circle on the horizon. Zaden scoops up the woman in the bright purple pants and spreads his glorious midnight wings. The strong downdraft blows my copper hair across my face and brings his forest lily scent, then they're away.

He's flying her to safety faster than any horse.

The leading group of runners has disappeared below ground. I catch up to a man with gray stubble on his chin. He lags and slumps onto the sand, almost lost in the mist of evaporating snow.

I stop beside him and tug his hand. "Come on. We're almost there. Get up."

He crawls a foot or two, then lies on the ground. I pull his hand, shouting. "Get up. The underground is right there!"

Zaden flies back and lands beside me. With a quick glance at me, he scoops up the fallen man and flies him to safety.

Lazius flies back too, plucks a struggling man off the sand, and whisks him ahead to safety.

I slow to a walk, keeping my eye on the place where the angels disappeared underground so I can stay on track. But my lungs are burning, and I can't run anymore.

Zaden and Lazius return twice more to pluck stragglers from the ground and fly them ahead. I finally reach them and head down a steep narrow tunnel, the temperature dropping with every yard. The tunnel opens out to a vast cavern that is almost empty.

"Where is everybody?" I ask Zaden, who kneels over a gasping woman, the one in the purple pants.

He nods toward the back of the cavern. "There are underground tunnels that take us a few miles further south. Lazius has followed the others." He studies the woman on the ground.

"Can you help her?"

Not so long ago, Zaden called mortals insects with a lifespan so short they were not worth caring about. Now he's asking me to save the life of a woman he doesn't even know.

I haven't used my healing powers in a long time. I've been so filled with anger and focused on my torturing powers.

But I'll try.

I fall to my knees beside Zaden, place my hands on the woman's forehead and belly, and then close my eyes. She's hot, and I suck out the excess heat from her body, drawing it out through my hands and releasing it into the air around me, feeling her limbs cool beneath my touch.

Her eyes flutter open, and she figures out what happened. "Thank you."

A spark of the person I used to be zaps through me. I used to work in the underwing, healing people. When did that all change? How did I lose sight of myself and become someone entirely different?

Zaden fetches the woman some water, and I move on to the next body. Of the five runners Zaden and Lazius rescued, I save three. That's two people who died because I asked Mahari for help.

Will they be added to the tally of deaths on my soul? Am I responsible for their lives as surely as if I plunged a dagger into their hearts?

Tears roll down my cheeks and drip from my chin. I wipe a hand across my snotty nose, but there's no stopping the outpouring of tears.

A great bubbling of sadness engulfs me. Not just for these two lives lost, but for my mom, my dad, Leo's betrayal, Leesa's death, but mainly for the person I used to be.

I will never be able to recapture the innocence I once had, the selfless desire to make the world a better place. I'm so far beyond that now. And innocence isn't something you can ever get back.

Zaden kneels beside me and pulls me into his arms. I'm a grown-ass woman, taller and bigger than most human men, but being cradled in Zaden's lap and having my hair stroked feels wonderful.

I run a hand down his black shirt, and some grains of sand grit my fingers. "How do you always know exactly what I need?"

He strokes my hair and kisses my temple. "I just know what *I* need. And right now, I need to hold you because you're hurting."

That's the perfect thing to say, and I nuzzle into his neck and sag against him, letting him support my weight completely.

My sadness ebbs away, finally, but I stay with my angel for long minutes, enjoying being in the one place where I can truly relax. My fingers play with his soft black shirt, and I breathe in his salty floral scent.

But it can't last forever. I wipe my tears and get to my feet, then tug him up after me, catching a sign of weariness on his face. "We'd better get going, or we'll get lost."

He slings the woman in the purple pants over one shoulder and the gray-bearded man over his other, but a new voice behind us speaks. "They stay here."

I spin around. An older man with heavy wrinkles, black eyes, brown skin, and a shaved head watches us from the shadows. "The desert will not allow these three to pass. You may leave them here with me, and I will see to their safety."

Zaden seems happy enough with that, but I need more information. "How? They can't make it back to Desert's Maw.

Will they live in this cave for the rest of their lives?"

The old Nashanti blinks. "They will choose their own paths. Some might choose to shave their heads and join the Nashanti. Some might choose to train and get fitter and stronger then attempt the return journey. Some might choose to die."

That sounds so harsh that I look for words to disagree with, but he's correct. They will choose their own paths, and this old man seems to have the wisdom to help them.

Zaden tugs on my arm. "Come on. We have to go."

I look into the old man's eyes, the unblinking black depths, and find neither generosity nor malice. I can only take him at his word. "Look after them."

"They will look after themselves," the man says.

I follow Zaden's pull and let him encourage me into a slow jog through the tunnel. We were never in danger of getting lost because only one path was carved through the stone. A few openings along the way lead to Nashanti living areas, but the way forward is evident.

After six or seven hours, we finally reach the large cavern at the other end of the tunnel. The few vestiges among the group glow brightly in the gloom, and lanterns on the cavern's perimeter flicker against the red rock walls. The smell of burning oxen blubber from the torches is thick, reminding me of home in the Undercity.

But this ain't the Undercity. It's a gathering of warriors, grouped around small fires, roasting food that the strongest and fastest among them carried in packs from Desert's Maw.

Quiet alertness simmers through the cavern, and our arrival barely causes a stir. We receive a few nods and an invitation to join some folks around a fire and eat reheated bread and dried meat.

Zaden refuses food, but I'm ravenous and gobble my portion down. Zaden wanders away to a snowmelt catch, then returns and hands me a mug of deliciously cold water.

I grin up at him, accepting the drink. "We made it."

Our Nashanti guide, sitting across the fire, blows a low whistle. "We have nowhere near made it yet."

Scarla

I'm used to weird sleep cycles. In the Undercity, I alternated between sleeping in the night hub with Dad and the day hub with Leo. So when Saheel tells us to try to catch some Z's, I'm the first asleep.

I wake a few hours later, nestled against Zaden, using his shoulder as a pillow. That must be giving him a numb hand.

I shift off him, but he cradles me closer and tucks me against his long hard body. I rest a hand on his tight abdomen and run it in lazy circles, pushing up the fabric of his shirt to reach the skin underneath.

I allow a trickle of Gaze through, just enough so his body glows lightly in the dark cave. All the fires are out, and just one lantern burns on the far wall, so nobody can see what's happening. Except me.

I run my hand across his belly, then higher, slowly tracing the ridges of his muscles, which are impressive even when they're loose with sleep.

"Careful, Scarla," he murmurs huskily.

His pants are tenting, and I can't help it. I put a hand down over his crotch and stroke him through the fabric.

The feel of him hard and yearning beneath my hand makes my thighs clench and my toes curl, and need grows between my legs.

We're surrounded by people, softly snoring and snuffling. Chances are at least a dozen are still awake, just lying still, but they can't see us.

Still, their presence is enough to stop me from doing what I really want: to un-button Zaden's pants, then roll on top and ride him slowly.

I make do with running my hand up his length and pressing my breasts against his side.

He grabs my ass and squeezes, and a quiet breathy moan escapes me.

"Lift your knee for me, mortal."

I raise my leg, giving him access to me from behind. His arm is long enough to reach me, but I must press close against him. His hand slips along my slick pussy, and he pushes a finger on my clit, hard.

Fuck, this feels good. So damn good.

With one hand, I fumble open his pants to free his cock, and my hand contacts his smooth hot skin at the same instant that he plunges fingers inside me.

I have to concentrate on not crying out, not moaning his name, and keeping my panting to a minimum. It's hard. Bloody hard.

I roll pre-cum around the head of his cock, and he shivers, making me even wetter.

My whole body is flush against his side, leaning into him, my breasts rubbing against his firm flesh while his fingers devour me, stroking, pressing, and circling in all the places I need.

He turns his head and claims my lips, whispering into my mouth, "Come for me, Scarla."

I stifle a scream and arch into him as my pleasure peaks, and he shudders with me, coming apart under my fingers.

I love him so much it fucking hurts.

He tenses under me. I look up into his eyes, which still glow black from his desire. "Are you ready to go again? That was quick," I joke.

He's staring over my shoulder across the cave, on full alert. I swivel to see what he's looking at. No glow, so no angel. "There's nobody there," I whisper.

Then I see it. A patch of darkness, blacker than the surrounding cave, moving slowly through the sleeping forms. It isn't human. No creature of earth swallows darkness the way this beast does, picking its way through the horizontal crowd.

Zaden puts a finger to my lips, and I know better than to ask a question or make any noise whatsoever. But if this thing is celestial, it can hear my pounding heart and smell my fear.

Zaden cleans close and whispers into my ear, barely audible. "Demon."

Maker-be-damned. The demon must be here for Zaden. He made that stupid bloodbond with the Xerxes fuckwit centuries ago, and he only broke it because the most recent fuckwit tried to kidnap me and deliver me to Angel VanDyke.

Now the demon has come to claim the price of breaking the bloodbond.

The dark figure flashes toward us so fast it's a blur, but Zaden is just as quick. He rolls us out of the way, and the demon strikes the sleeper behind us.

The man's screams are bloodcurdling, and my skin jumps up in goose flesh.

Fire and fury light up the cavern, and the other sleepers jolt awake, alert and terrified, some of them screaming too.

The demon is visible now, with the flames licking its body. It is pure black and looks like an overgrown bat, with large black leathery wings, matted fur, and oversized fangs. It beats its wings and hovers above us, holding its victim by the neck.

The demon chews into the victim, tearing off one limb at a time and consuming them.

The sounds of hells below fill the cavern, howls and screams. Horror fills me as I peer into the dancing flames above the crowd. The man's face is played out in flame and fire, a macabre light show of a human being tortured.

"What the fuck is that?" I spit.

"That's a glimpse of our friend's future in hell."

Torture scenes continue to play above us in flames, reflecting off the cavern's rocky ceiling and walls. The image that burns strongest is the man's face contorted in agony.

I don't even have time to feel bad about it, although maybe I should—this is another death that wouldn't have happened if I was never born.

But all I can think about is Zaden. If he hadn't rolled us out of the way, the demon would have caught him, and it would be his agonized face seared in flames above us.

"We have to go." I grab Zaden's hand and try to pull him, but he is a rock, a mountain, immovable. "Zaden, we have to go. Now."

"It's too late."

The flames above us flicker out because the demon has consumed the last of the warrior's flesh. But his torture will continue in hells below for eternity.

Maybe the demon will leave now. Maybe it thinks it's paid off the bloodbond debt. Maybe it believes that victim was Zaden?

My hopes plummet when red flames dance in the demon's eyes, and it locks them directly on Zaden.

Zaden

The demon disappears into the inky blackness near the cave's ceiling.

"Light more lanterns," somebody calls.

I can sense the demon's presence lurking nearby. With a rush of wind, it swoops from the air and lands beside me, claws scraping against the cave wall, its black beady eyes filled with malice. The stink of burning flesh and brimstone surrounds it.

The humans scatter, leaving open rocky ground for us to battle.

The demon lunges and its claws grip my head, so close I can smell the rotting. A clump of hair pulls into its mouth, and it squeals with delight. Its wings, leathery and moist, flap against my face.

I parry the demon's attack with my sword, and the screech of metal echoes throughout the cave. The demon is fast, but I'm faster. I strike it with a quick blow to its side, and it staggers before regaining its footing and lunging at me again.

I dodge the demon's attack, channeling my anger into my sword. The creature counters with a burst of flames, but I shield myself with my wings, gritting my teeth against the pain of the flames licking my feathers.

With a strong beat of its wings, the demon takes to the air, the sound of the wings flapping and scuttling on the rock wall like a million skitter beetles.

Lanterns have been lit, so I can follow the hell beast's movements through the cave. It swoops down, its black wings beating furiously as it screeches in anger.

I grip Ashmodu tightly and take to the air in pursuit, dodging its sharp claws as they reach for me.

Lazius shows his golden wings, earning gasps from the humans who didn't know he was an angel. He doesn't have a sword, so I don't know what he can do other than distract and annoy the demon, but I'll take it. His usual lazy grin is replaced by grim determination as he pounds his wings and joins the airborne battle.

The demon ignores Lazius, keeping its laser focus on me. I'm the one who shattered a bloodbond, so I'm the target of its fury.

Scarla's voice penetrates the slashing and screeching sounds of battle. "Lazius. Here!" She tosses her celestial-tipped dagger in a high arc, and the blond angel hauls ass to catch it midair. It isn't as effective as a sword, but it's better than nothing.

I swing my sword, striking the demon's chest. It roars in pain but quickly recovers, lashing at me with its tail. I manage to dodge, but Lazius is not so lucky; the demon's tail catches him across the face and sends him crashing to the rocky ground.

Scarla helps Lazius to his feet. Blood streams down his face, but he still manages a weak smile. "I'm fine," he says, "Let's get this Maker-fucker."

I lift my sword, preparing for the demon's next attack, but the monster swoops off to the side, where it lands on an outcropping of rock. It paces back and forth, its rancid body swaying from side to side, its wings spread out behind it, threatening to whip and strike us if we dare come close.

Lazius leans on Scarla for support, scowling at his tiny dagger. "Remind me to bring my sword next time."

The demon takes to the air, and I have to meet it. Have to keep it away from the mortals, away from Scarla. I strike again, but Ashmodu clatters uselessly off its impenetrable hide.

The fucking demon doesn't fall. It shrugs off our attacks, its claws and teeth tearing at us as we fight to keep it at bay.

I lag and lurch, my body bruised and battered.

With a supernaturally fast lunge, the demon grabs hold of my left wing in its sharp teeth and tears, ripping feathers and flesh. Pain shoots through my wing. I grit my teeth, struggling to keep up with the demon.

My arms ache from swinging Ashmodu, and my body gets heavier and heavier from the effort of staying in the air as my blood drips onto the rock floor.

But the pain in my wing is all-encompassing. With each beat of my wings, it stabs through my body, a white-hot knife piercing my flesh, making it hard to focus on anything else.

I catch a glimpse of Scarla standing in front of the other humans, studying the battle, probably looking for any weaknesses in the demon or the opportunity to strike with Inflict without hurting me or Lazius.

Finally, after what feels like an eternity, I see an opening. I seize it, plunging my sword deep into the demon's chest. Ashmodu buzzes under my grip as it strikes true, and the monster lets out a bloodcurdling scream.

I wait for the hell beast to crumple to the cave floor or turn into smoke and ash, but it just sags. It recovers quickly, too damn quickly, its wings beating furiously as it rises into the air.

I just struck the bloody thing right through the heart—if it even has one—and it didn't die. Ashmodu is a celestial blade, the only weapon that can kill an angel.

But apparently it can't kill a demon. Fuck.

The demon hovers above the crowd of humans, darts down, plucks one in its sharp talons, and returns to the air.

I scan for Scarla, my heart hammering. She's still on the rocky ground, thank fuck. Alive, for now.

The demon devours the poor mortal, regenerating its energy. Flames dance around the devil, flickering off its bat wings, portraying the torture and agony of the man it consumes. The fire dances quickly, pulsing with the demon's heartbeat, flickering reds, oranges, and yellows painting a picture of the man's eternal damnation.

It wasn't Scarla this time, but it could be next time. I have to lead the demon away from the cave. Away from Scarla.

I lock eyes with Lazius, who nods. I fly upward, leading the hell beast outside into the open desert. Agony lances through my wing, and I don't know how far or how fast I will be able to fly. Lazius follows, thank the Maker. He batters and attacks the demon from behind, keeping its attention scattered, keeping me alive.

We fly for what feels like hours under the beating sun, the demon lunging at me, Lazius poking at the monster, and me struggling to remain airborne, just wanting to lure the thing as far as possible away from Scarla.

I fly higher and higher, leading the demon away from the cave, but the pain in my left wing intensifies with each beat.

Finally, we reach the desert's edge. This will have to do. I land messily in the rocky foothills of the mountains outside Malanox. Like charcoal, the rocks are black and smooth, and the vegetation is a withering brown. No color, no life, just the blistering sun and heat radiating off the stone and sand.

The demon screeches and lunges at us, but Lazius and I fight back with fucking fury.

Metal rings, and the demon's black blood coats Ashmodu, its acrid stench filling my nostrils.

The beast of hell lunges at me, and I dart aside. I toss Ashmodu to Lazius, who grabs the sword from the air and plunges it into the demon's chest.

Finally, it is wounded. It can regenerate by feeding on a human's soul, but no mortals are nearby. For now, it is injured badly enough to retreat into the shadows, disappearing between craggy outcrops.

I slump to the ground, my left wing throbbing. I take deep breaths, trying to calm my racing heart and ignore the pain.

"Come on, dude, we need to get away from here." Lazius pulls me to my feet, and I lean on his shoulder. We've defeated the demon for now, but it will return. It will hound me until I repay my blood debt.

I've learned something important—the demon feasts on humans to recover its energy. So while the demon hunts me, I cannot return to Scarla's side. I cannot risk her precious life.

Scarla

We leave the tunnel at the break of dusk when the sand under-foot is still hot enough to burn. I wear my thick ox-hide boots that protect the soles of my feet, but some runners will earn blistered feet.

I could lend someone my boots, but they are my most precious possession. At least, they used to be. They were the only memento I had from my mom when I thought she was dead. Now that she's alive, they don't mean nearly as much.

My most precious possession is probably the celestial-tipped dagger that Zaden gifted me, one of the only weapons that can kill an angel. If he'd known I would use it to kill Belial and become the Cloaked Queen, he might never have given it to me.

The desert in the distance is brighter than behind us, with more of that blinding glow I always experience when I fly across it. Perhaps the sand is whiter in the desert center and reflects the sun more strongly.

Apparently this stretch is more brutal than the last one. It's the same distance, but dusk is shorter, so we have less time to complete it. A few slower runners chose to stay in the cavern overnight to rest and will attempt the run tomorrow at dawn.

I take a deep breath and sprint into the daylight. I glance at the sky, looking for specks that might be Zaden or Lazius. Why the fuck haven't they come back?

I need to focus on the crossing. My heart pounds in my chest, and soon my legs ache from the exertion. The other humans run alongside me, their faces twisted in determination as we approach the next shelter.

The sun is setting, and I can feel the temperature dropping with each passing moment. We have to make it to the cave before nightfall, or runners will freeze to death. I glance up at the sky, watching as the sun dips lower below the horizon. We don't have much time.

My mind races as I run, always reverting to the fucking angel and why he hasn't returned. I'm going to kill him when I see him.

The wind whips through my hair, and sand stings my face. But I don't stop. I keep running, pushing myself to go faster, to go farther.

Finally, I see the cave up ahead, a small opening in the rock, our only hope. I sprint harder, my heart racing as I hear the other humans pounding across the sand behind me.

As we reach the cave's entrance, I turn around and look back at the desert. The sun has set, and the cold is already seeping into my bones. But everybody made it. We are safe for now.

I step inside the cave and collapse onto the ground, gasping for breath. I close my eyes and try to calm my racing heart. But I can't relax entirely until I lock eyes with Zaden.

* * *

Night falls, and the Desert Mawkers light ox-blubber fires in the cave, bringing a familiar oily and smoky smell and a cozy atmosphere. Flames dance brightly against the walls, casting rivulets of golden light throughout the cavern. But a brighter light shines in from the cave entrance.

"Can you see that?" I ask the nearest Desert Mawker but get nothing but a grunt and a shake of the head.

I cross to the cave's mouth, and the glow brightens, shining from the horizon with magic so strong it is blinding. Without even thinking, I wander out of the cave and into the freezing night. I pull my shirt close about my body for warmth, for comfort and blink rapidly so the water in my eyes doesn't stiffen.

I have to investigate that glow. I dial my Gaze down to almost nothing so I'm not blinded and walk across the fresh, open sand.

I finally reach the source of the glow. It is a structure. The air around it shimmers with otherworldly energy. A strange sensation washes over me as I approach it, like an electric current. I squint against the light, my eyes watering, and suddenly, I see it clearly. The gate to heaven, glowing brightly with magical energy that only I can see.

Holy Hades. The gate to heaven, right here in the middle of the desert. I step closer, and its energy vibrates right through me. I can sense the ancient magic woven into its fabric, and my mouth falls open. Awe and wonder wash through me.

Instinctively, I turn to share this with Zaden. This is why he kidnapped me, so he could use my Gaze to find the entrance to heaven itself, and I want to share this moment with him, but he isn't here.

The others in the cave can't share this with me, they're just huddling in the hidey-hole, shivering in the cold desert air. They're so focused on survival that they can't imagine the possibility of something greater beyond this world.

But I can see it, clear as day. The gate to heaven, beckoning me with its brilliant light. A sense of urgency rises within me as if I'm meant to step through that gate, to journey beyond this world and into the next. It calls to me. I take a step forward, then another, following the pull.

But I can't go, I'm not permitted there. I laugh hollowly. I've found the one thing Zaden has been searching for these past centuries, and it calls to me like a magnet to my soul, urging me through. But I'm not welcome in heaven.

And if I tell Zaden I've found it, I will lose him. He will pass through to his otherworldly home, leaving me alone. I'm not selfless enough to let him go.

Scarla

The desert is a harsh bitch. But she's also fair, not discriminating against anyone. There is something immediate and meditative about the urgency of sprinting over sand as fast as you can every dawn and dusk.

The main group has finally made it to the last hidey-hole, a small dugout where we stand shoulder to shoulder and breathe each other's air so we can fit.

We're only three miles to Malanox and will make it there at dusk.

I can't think why Zaden hasn't returned. The only reason that makes any sense is that he's too injured to fly, and I keep picturing him bleeding out in the desert somewhere, his blood seeping into the thirsty sand.

I shake that thought aside. It won't help anyone if I fall to pieces. But the answer is just three miles away, and I can't wait until dusk.

I shimmy through the crowded warriors, wriggling toward the exit. I'll scout ahead and prepare the castle for the Desert Mawkers' arrival, I tell myself. But really, I just need answers.

Where is Zaden? Why didn't he return to help us through the desert? Is he injured? Is he dead?

Lazius too. He hasn't returned either, which worries me. I

didn't mind torturing him a few weeks ago, but now the thought of him in pain has me on edge.

The Desert's Maw warriors watch as I climb out the hole in the ceiling that marks the exit. They are used to me going outside at odd hours, but they still stare as I go.

From above, the cavern looks like a hole in the ground, a desert fox burrow. Maybe that's what it originally was, and it's just been widened by the Nashanti.

Days of running and poor sleep have worn me out, and the sun beating down on me doesn't help. There is no water out here—at least none I can find without a Nashanti guide—so I focus on putting one foot in front of the other and try to keep my mind off my parched mouth and my fear for Zaden.

My energy is flagging when I finally see the smudge of brown in the distance, beyond the red sand. Thermo-oxen graze on the brown grass, moving lazily under the hot sun. Their thick hides insulate them from the extreme temperatures and are useful for protecting buildings. With so little food out here, they scavenge and graze twenty hours a day.

Usually, I give them a wide berth. They're not dangerous but massive and have been known to accidentally trample kids. But I'm too tired to go around, so I plow through. The tops of their backs are at my shoulders, and their heads and horns are even higher. They smell of soil and manure, and their munching and chewing on the meager brown grass is noisy.

I head through the thermo-oxen grazing land and into Hightown, where the richest of the rich in Malanox live. They live in high buildings aboveground with thick insulation. I used to think they were the epitome of style, absolutely drowning in wealth, but since I've been to Solren and inside several angels' castles, their homes no longer look so magnificent.

Especially since skitter beetles, each as large as my thermo-oxen boots, scuttle along the streets and up the stone walls, kings under the sun. By dusk, they'll all be gone.

I shudder and look for the dim glow that coats their shells. Humans have a glowing light that runs down their spine which I can snap with the force of my mind, although I've been relying on Inflict this past month. For these beetles, the shine coats their carapace super dimly, but I take comfort in the knowledge that I can kill any that get too close with just a thought.

I come to the bridge over the river. This is the spot where I first realized the dangerous stranger who visited Fra Perkins' deathbed in the Undercity was actually the Margrave of Malanox. Zaden.

I cross the bridge and nod at the guards in the sentry box, who nod back. They haven't seen me in months, but they are used to me coming and going at all times of the day, so they let me pass without a challenge.

Malanox castle. I used to think Malanox castle was grand and luxurious, with its turret in each corner and ornate wooden front doors. But compared with the other places I've been, it's positively frugal, and I can see now what Zaden means when he says he lives a simple life. It all depends on your perspective.

I dart up the outside stairs and charge through the front doors, calling for Zaden.

The entrance foyer is just as I remember. Impressively large, with a double-high ceiling that stretches to infinity. Most torches on the walls are unlit, making me think the master isn't in his castle.

I ignore the grand marble staircase sweeping up and splitting, with hardwood banisters and marble treads. I let the red and gold carpets flash beneath my feet and push through into the servants' corridors, which are narrower and duller. No angel in sight.

I haul ass to the northwest tower, then climb the stairs two at a time and burst into Zaden's bedroom, calling his name desperately.

No response.

The bed doesn't look slept in, although the castle full of servants quickly tidies a rumpled sheet. There are forest lilies on his bedside table, so he's been here recently, although they are browning and lacing the air with a sweet rotting smell. The view out the window catches my eye. From here, I can see Penngrove Forest, where the lilies come from, and the Dead Desert, which has been my home for the past two weeks.

I sit on his bed and sag, my exhaustion hitting bone deep. It is plush with a vibrant bedcover, but it is empty.

A light tap at the door has my heart in my throat, but it's just a servant. The woman is short with generous curves and fear-filled eyes. Her long ponytail flaps against her back as she scurries into the room.

"Hello, Abby."

She bobs a curtsy and avoids my gaze. "Hello, milady."

She's the maid who was assigned to me after Molly disappeared. No, after Molly died. She has none of Molly's spark and vigor, and I've failed at every attempt to make her my friend. Now I just accept her curtsies and miladies and look for friends elsewhere.

"The Margrave isn't here, milady. He left a week ago."

"Was he injured?"

"Yes, milady. He arrived with a wound, but it healed before he left."

I sag deeper into the mattress. I'm glad he is better, but why in hells below didn't he come back to the desert? Or maybe he did. Maybe he's flying overhead looking for me right now.

"Where did he go?"

She dips another curtsy. "The Margrave packed a bag and took one of the carriages, milady. I'm afraid I don't know where he's gone."

Oh. One doesn't pack a bag and take a carriage into the Dead Desert, so he must've gone south. Probably to Solren.

I sigh. I suppose he had a good reason for pissing off to Solren instead of saving the lives of desert runners. He'd better, or he'll be in all sorts of trouble.

I drag myself off the bed and out of the room. Being in here without Zaden is just depressing. Besides, I need to wash and refresh, and I know just the place. I wind down the stairs to the first floor, duck out of the servants' hallways, back into the main foyer, and then circle around to the central staircase. This is the only set of stairs leading to the underground pool, precisely where I need to be.

I descend the stairs and immediately feel calmer. As I go deeper, the air becomes thicker and filled with the smell of damp stone that reminds me of my childhood.

I'm in a subterranean cavern beneath the castle. A peaceful pool bubbles up from underneath the rock and trickles away in a stream that disappears beneath the castle walls, keeping it cool during the day. The clear, cool water seems to sparkle in the blue light

I take off my filthy clothes and amble into the water, following the gentle slope of the ground. The water is too cold for any of the staff to use, but it's refreshing and delightful for me and exactly what I need.

I submerge myself completely, watching the pale blue light

shimmer and blur beneath the water's surface, and I stay down long enough that when I come out, I'm gasping for air.

Last time I was here, my relationship with Zaden was in a complicated phase, to say the least. I hated him and loved him, and he felt something like the same toward me. But it didn't stop us from having the hottest sex of my life.

I miss him so much. I haven't seen him in a week. I'm glad he is okay, so fucking glad. But I still miss the ever-living hells out of him.

After a short cry and a long soak, I emerge from the underground lake dripping and refreshed. I call for a towel, and Abby darts down and hands me one, then disappears just as fast. I swear, that girl thinks I am a dragon when all I want to be is her friend.

I dress in some clean clothes—a glorious, clean blue shirt and tan pants—then prepare the castle for the hundreds of warriors who will soon arrive.

The servants whip into a flurry of activity, preparing guestrooms in the castle and bunks in the guards' barracks out back. Some Desert Mawkers will sleep on the floors, but plush carpets are much more comfortable than rocky caves, so I'm sure they won't mind too much.

They will arrive by dusk's end. Some stragglers will come over the next few days, the ones who chose to stay an extra day or night in some cave to regenerate their strength before the next desert stretch, but we'll still need to accommodate hundreds of extra bodies in less than an hour.

Mahari is one of the first to arrive. I hadn't realized she was so fast because I was always one of the last. I pace impatiently while she showers and changes and gulps down some food, then I tell her we're going to Solren.

"It can wait until tomorrow, Scar. I'm exhausted," she grumbles.

I want to scream in frustration. "Your warriors can wait until tomorrow. They can walk or stroll or crawl, for all I care. There are plenty of places to shelter between here and Solren. But you and I can take a horse and carriage and get there in a few hours. We can be the advance party. Your sister has no idea we're coming, so we should arrive early to tell her what to expect. We don't even know if she can accommodate all your people, she may need some time to sort that out."

It's true that Bwadu doesn't know we will arrive tomorrow, although she knows we will come at some stage. But my real impatience is a burning desire to see Zaden. I suspect that's where he's gone, so I'll track him and kiss his perfect damn lips, even if he's in the middle of the world's most important conversation.

I just want to kiss my angel...and then win this Maker-be-damned war.

Mahari nods slowly, and it's all I can do not to run around and shake her shoulders. "Fine," she finally says after long deliberation. "That's a good plan. I can sleep after I speak with Bwadu."

"Good! Let's go."

The ox-hide insulated carriage is kept inside, so we can access it day or night. Ten minutes later, Bwadu and I are inside the carriage, along with one of her top men, a short wiry warrior with green eyes and a pleasant grin. He doesn't have the glow of a vestige, but I've seen that face turned feral with determination while running, and I imagine he's formidable in battle.

I swear, these carriages have something against me. They bump and batter my ass and smack me in the side of the head more times than I can count. I even thump the carriage back at one point, but it doesn't make it behave any better.

After a couple hours of the carriage inflicting me, we arrive in Solren.

The most privileged members of Solren live in the enclosed section, protected by the temperature seal. It is on an elevated platform in the middle of the city. Access to this area is only granted via the Rim Road, which winds around the sealed city's circumference, marking its boundary. It spirals up, rising fifty feet above its starting point.

We pass through the official checkpoint at the Rim Road's base without challenge, then wind up to the sealed city proper.

We alight from the carriage just inside the temperature-controlled sealed section. I ask the driver to keep going so as not to draw attention to why a fine carriage is stopping at the outskirts of respectable suburbia.

Bwadu's lair is tucked underneath the raised city, so it's protected by the sorcered dome but still hidden from society. It is literally underground.

I spot the worn stone steps that lead down to a maintenance tunnel. Nestled beneath the city's walls, hidden away beside the winding road, are a series of buildings crammed next to one another. Tucked between archways supporting the road that rises around and above us, the dwellings are covered in dirt and grime.

A maintenance worker dressed in gray overalls is leaning against the wall, reeking of alcohol. His muscles are toned, though, and his posture hints at his alertness. His skin has a dimmed, corrupted shade of blyberry blue, the hue I know represents a vestige with the power of Lapse. He's trying to look like a drunk, but he's the guard on duty.

As we approach, his vestigial Lapse power repels me, making me weaker with every step I take. I hate the feeling of my strength leaking away. I've grown accustomed to the swirling of Gaze and Inflict, and I feel empty and alone without them.

Clearly, the guard doesn't recognize me. He makes no attempt to let us pass.

Some of my familiar anger and entitlement rise within me, and my first impulse is to inflict him with pain so he steps aside. But with a deep breath, I stifle that instinct and use my words instead. "I am Scar Rosedarter Healer from Malanox. This is General Mahari Nuldarter from Desert's Maw, sister of General Bwadu Nuldarter. Let us pass."

The man with the bruised-blyberry glow nods, then moves far enough away that we can pass without my powers weakening.

We go down some stairs and turn around, taking the path below the maintenance tunnel and deeper into the hidden houses. The walls alternate between rock and wood like we're passing through different structures and caves.

And then, we enter a large room with a low ceiling and long walls. Inside are tables and chairs and a group of people relaxing, but they jump to their feet at our arrival.

Mahari and Bwadu lock eyes across the room, and electricity tingles between them. They come from a family of revolutionaries, and I know Mahari left her sister to gather support across the desert, and now they are finally reunited.

They dart toward each other and wrap each other in a warm, hard hug.

I'm not a crier, but tears spring to my eyes. I miss Leesa so fucking much. I would do anything to be given one last chance to throw my arms around her and squeeze her tight, to caress her blue-black hair and see her toothy grin. She brought me so much joy as a child, always looking out for me, always making me laugh. She shouldered responsibility so I had the freedom to muck up and explore the Undercity, sneaking into tunnels I shouldn't be in and coming back at night to regale her with stories of my exploration.

Mahari and Bwadu don't release each other for a long, long time.

Zaden

I dive into the crystal clear waters of the Broken Ocean, my wings tucked tightly against my back. The Seer told me I must swim across the widest ocean to find the Ring of Roth, so I am.

The ocean is vast and deep, and the cold water seeps into my bones. But I am a Fallen Angel with powers beyond mortal comprehension. I am not afraid of the water but wary of creatures lurking beneath the surface.

I swim for hours, my eyes scanning the water for any sign of danger, any signs of the Ring. The sun beats down on my back, turning the top layer into steam, but the heat does not bother me.

As I swim, my mind wanders to Scarla. I hope she has the good sense to avoid the angels and stay away from Solren. She will be safe in Malanox, surrounded by the Desert Maw warriors. But sadly, good sense is one thing that infuriating woman lacks.

The thought of Scarla drives me forward, and I swim faster. The ocean seems to go on forever, but I do not falter. I will find the Ring of Roth, no matter what it takes.

As the sun begins to set, I spot something in the distance. A glimmering object, barely visible in the fading light. Could it be the Ring? My heart rate picks up.

Swimming towards the glimmering object, I sense something

is off. It isn't the Ring, but something else entirely. A creature lurking in the deep, its scales glinting under the fading sun.

A Kraken. A giant sea monster with tentacles as thick as tree trunks. The Kraken is furious and hungry, and its tentacles lash at me, knocking me off course. I dive deeper into the water, trying to dodge the attacks, but it follows me relentlessly.

I draw my sword and prepare to strike the Kraken, but it's much larger than I expected, and Ashmodu barely dents its thick skin. A slimy tentacle wraps around me, squeezing the air out of my lungs. I gasp for breath and struggle to break free.

My strength is fading. I'm running out of time. I focus all my energy on one final strike, aiming for the Kraken's eye. My sword connects with a sickening squish, and the Kraken lets out a deafening roar.

I break free from the Kraken's grip and swim to the surface, gasping for air. The creature doesn't follow. Good. But the Maker-be-damned Ring of Roth is nowhere to be seen.

* * *

I take a deep breath and look at the mountain peak towering above me. Blue Mountain is the tallest mountain in the world, and according to the Seer, the Ring of Roth should be hidden somewhere at the summit. I flex my wings and ascend.

I soar higher and higher up the mountain, my wings beating with effortless power. But as I ascend, the air grows thinner, and my breathing becomes labored.

Finally, the air becomes too thin, and I am forced to land on a rocky outcropping. I continue my ascent on foot, my eyes scanning the terrain for any sign of the Ring of Roth. The climb is treacherous, and I slip and stumble more than once. But I refuse to give up.

As I climb higher, the wind picks up, and snow layers the ground. The mountain is treacherous, and I turn my thoughts from Scarla, where they usually are, to every step I take, careful not to slip and fall. I don't want to end up bleeding and injured at the base of the damn mountain with no ring to show for my efforts.

After hours of climbing, I reach the summit. I search everywhere, turning over every rock and digging under the snow. No fucking ring. I have crossed the hottest desert, swum the widest ocean, and climbed the tallest mountain, and I still haven't found the Maker-be-damned ring.

Curse that drunken Seer. She's clearly full of shit.

Scarla

I stride through the city streets, needing time to clear my mind. The more people we recruit to our cause, the heavier the burden of responsibility weighs on my shoulders.

Mahari, Bwadu, Lazius, even Zaden...they all expect me to rule. But I've lost confidence in my ability to make good decisions. The power roiling through my veins makes me careless and reckless, a bad combination for a Queen.

So, once again, I'm headed away from the group to find some space. Once I could count my friends on one finger, now I have more than I know what to do with. My friends list has grown too long, and I need time alone.

I wander through the streets of Solren, enjoying the feeling of getting lost. The sun is low in the sky, so people will soon fill the streets. But for now, I have the place to myself.

A scuffle beside me stops me in my tracks. They don't have skitter beetles this far south, and not much else can survive outdoors during the day...unless a thermo ox is hiding under that trash can lid.

My heart hammers. Despite the power coursing through me, I'm still vulnerable to attack. The plummeting stone in Desert's Maw proved that—I can be squished as easily as the next person.

A bright light catches my eye. Its orange-white ethereal glow should be beautiful, but it is terrifying. The angel is dressed for battle. Most of these assholes wear the latest fashion, with long sleeves and high-cut collars, but this male looks straight from the history books, clad in black armor and wielding a sword that shines with an unearthly fire. Magnificent yet fucking terrifying.

I throw a spear of pain at the angel, then turn and sprint. My feet pound against the cobblestone streets as I run through the city. My heart thunders in my chest, and my breath comes in ragged gasps. Behind me, the sounds of pursuit are growing ever closer. Panic races through my veins, but I force myself to keep running, pushing my body to its limits.

The buildings blur into a wall of gray as I race through the shadows, my wild copper hair streaming behind me.

I glance over my shoulder and see more attackers joining the chase, angels, their eyes burning black with anger.

Too many. There are too many. I can't inflict them all at once, at least not for long.

A scream rises in my throat and rains down onto the cobblestones. Fallen Angels swarm in the streets ahead, drawn by the sound, closing in on me. Herding me.

Metal screeches against cobblestone as I skid to a halt. I'm surrounded. I spin in a slow circle, my heart racing while considering my options.

The angel draws closer, his eyes shining with malice as he takes in my fear. VanDyke. The cream-and-gold monster with a perfect cupid face, blond curls, a broad smile, and the faintest Z-shaped scar on his cheek. The angel who kidnapped and tormented me then dressed me up like a doll and took me to dinner.

I take a deep breath, feeling the flood of power still surging through my veins. I am not going down without a fight. I can't let them take me. I may sometimes bite off more than I can chew, but I've dealt with the impossible before.

"Hello, Scarla. How lovely to see you," he drawls.

Rage builds in my belly. This is the fuckwit who had me chased, kidnapped, and paraded, and now he's trying to ensnare me again. "Why don't you just kill me? I'm surrounded, and you're still not done talking?"

He stops in his tracks and stares at me with a curious expression. "You have a death wish? Interesting. But I haven't decided if I want Gaze or Inflict, so I can't kill you yet."

"You'll never have either, VanDyke."

"It's over, Scarla," he calls. "Why don't you come here and be a good girl? Come and live out your days with me in the lap of luxury. No need to skulk around the streets like a skitter beetle. You're better than that."

Smugness laces his words. The asshole has been plotting this for months. He's wanted to catch me, to own me. A world of shit is about to rain down on my head.

I once had nothing, but now I have friends, a home, and a future. I can't give all that up. I'm not ready to die, especially since I'm doomed for hells below. I've seen the scenes of torture flickering in flames in the cave while that demon consumed his victim, and I'm not ready to face that yet.

I take a step toward him, then another. VanDyke's smile deepens. He readies his sword. "That wasn't so hard, was it? Come to Papa."

I shake my head. "Come to Mama."

A confused expression passes over his face, then I launch myself. I inflict a spear of pain into his shoulder. VanDyke gasps and stumbles backward, losing his grip on his sword. The blade clatters against the cobblestones.

The other angels converge on me, their eyes glowing black with rage. They hunt me like lions, ready to tear into my flesh and spill my blood over the cobblestones.

I scan the buildings, desperate to find a place to hide. I launch into a flat-out sprint. Around a corner, I spy a narrow alley hidden in the darkness between two buildings. My heart leaps as I steal a quick glance behind me.

I might make it...at least I have to try. I whirl around, sprinting down the alley, my feet pounding the stones until they bleed. Each step takes an eternity, but I dare not slow, letting fear drive me ahead of the angels.

How can I outrun angels? They are faster, but terror gives me wings.

A surge of power courses through my veins as my familiar strength fills me, responding to the threat. Everything around me fades away as I feel my magic responding to the call of the Fallen Angels.

Out of time, I whirl around and face them.

The angels are taken aback, confused. The last time they saw me, at the Cloaked Council ball, I was weak. Since then, I've trained and learned and am a worthy opponent with complete control over my dyad.

One angel steps forward, his voice full of menace. A male I don't recognize with skin the color of coal and wings of ebony. His face is expertly carved, framed with perfectly-coiffed locks of hair, short enough to not obscure his vision.

"You are the one," he says. "The one who thinks she can be our Queen. But we will never allow an insect to rule us. You are no Queen—you are a prisoner. Mine."

My mouth goes dry, my heart racing in my chest. I summon Inflict to my command, hoping to hells I can keep all these angels under my control.

Before I can respond, a voice speaks from the shadows. The voice is deep, penetrating. It carries the weight of a mountain, quiet authority and calmness.

"No, Marlon," the voice says. "She is mine."

Zaden, his black wings spread wide and Ashmodu in his hand. I have never seen him so fierce, so determined. Black smoke swirls through his eyes, and his fists are clenched, trying to hold back his killing haze. He steps forward, his gaze fixed on his enemies.

The Fallen Angels step back. They must see something terrible in his face, acknowledge his ferocity and power. The sweat off his body, the scent of determination, all masked by the blood from his last fight.

Zaden's sword glows with a brilliant silvery purple light as he steps forward, and the Fallen Angels begin to retreat. Slowly, I move towards Zaden, my body quivering with power and fear.

He reaches out and grabs my hand, then pulls me tight. He pounds the cobblestones with his wings and takes flight, holding me fast against his chest, the Fallen Angels lost in the darkness below.

Zaden

Celestial blades are forged in the primordial fires, infused with the power of a thousand birthing suns, and the only things able to kill an angel. I thought they could destroy anything, but I was wrong.

I plunged Ashmodu right into that demon's chest, and all it did was slow him down. That one demon almost got the better of Lazius and me, two angels against one demon, and we barely made it out alive. It will keep coming until it has claimed my soul and dragged me to the fiery pits of hells below.

The demon replenishes its energy by consuming humans, so I can't let it anywhere near Scarla.

Maker-be-damned. That means I can't go anywhere near Scarla because I am a magnet to these demons.

I feel tugged in several directions. My goal for centuries has been to find the gates to heaven. More recently, I realized I need to recover the stolen Ring of Roth before I go to heaven; otherwise they'll boot me straight out again.

But none of those slight tugs is anything compared to the tidal wave pulling me toward Scarla. Every fiber of my being yearns for her. My soul has found its other half. She is in every waking thought and invades my dreams, so being away from her is torture.

I risked everything to swoop in and rescue her from the angels yesterday, but it may have drawn the demon's attention to her.

The only way I can keep her safe and be with her is to find a way to kill the demon.

And the only person who might know how to do that is at the Howling Cat.

Somebody has replaced the door on its hinges, and it sits straighter now but is still as grimy as shit. Inside, the tavern is dull and smoke-filled, and I swear they are playing the same droning song that was on last time.

The Seer is staring at the ox-hide curtains when I push through, as though she's been waiting for me. She's wearing the same leather jacket and oversized pants with rips showing her skinny white legs, and she still hasn't washed her hair.

She beams at me. "Perfect timing, angel. Oryan here has just poured your beer." She hooks a thumb at the barman, who slides a cold frothy ale across the counter.

"I suppose you've come to thank me," she says. Her slur is less pronounced than last time, so hopefully she'll be more coherent.

I sip the beer and try not to wince. It's cold, but it tastes like piss. "Surely you know exactly why I'm here, oh Oracle of Howlka," I deadpan.

She nods vigorously, and a strand of lanky hair whips her face. "Of course I do. You're here to pay my tab. Oryan here is threatening to cut me off, but I told him you'll pay for everything."

I raise an eyebrow. "Is that so? And how long has your bar tab been open?"

She grins cheekily. "Oh, about ten years."

I splutter and spray beer across the counter. I have plenty

of money, but the amount this woman drinks over ten years would be enough to bankrupt most people.

"Plus interest. Oryan has only kept me in booze for the past decade because I promised him all that interest."

I glance at Oryan to see if she's joking, but his expression is stern and expectant, his furry eyebrows knitted together above a granite face. "Cash only," he growls.

The Seer doesn't bother to look ashamed or even to plead. A smug smirk has settled over her face like she's pleased one of her long-term predictions is coming true.

"Fine," I growl. "But only if you can answer my question."

The bartender glances at the disheveled oracle with a small smile. "It happened exactly as you predicted," he says.

She brushes some imaginary dust off her leather jacket. "Of course."

I thump the bar to get their attention. "You haven't answered my question yet," I remind her.

She skulls an entire beer before slamming the glass on the table and demanding another. "Make it a double," she slurs.

The bartender frowns, probably trying to figure out what a double beer looks like.

I lean on the bar and immediately regret it because it's sticky. "Plus, you still owe me an answer on the Ring of Roth. You told me to climb the highest mountain, cross the hottest desert, and swim the widest ocean, and I did all that and still didn't find the Ring."

She giggles drunkenly, and a globule of spit flies from her lips and lands on my arm. "Did I say that? That's just one of those oracle things that sound really cool, you know. I didn't mean it."

My chest grows hot, and my eyes darken. I wipe away her spit from my arm. "You didn't mean it? But you told me oracles never lie."

She swats that away like a fly. "Oh, that was a lie. To find the Ring of Roth, you must return to where it all began." She giggles. "Sorry about the deserts and mountains and stuff, I must've been really drunk."

"And are you really drunk now?" I ask with warning in my voice.

"Always!" She raises her glass and takes another gulp.

She is the most infuriating Seer I've ever had the displeasure of meeting. To find the Ring of Roth, I didn't have to swim the Maker-be-damned ocean, I just had to return to where it all began.

I drink my beer in silence while I think about that, turning over the options in my head for what that might mean.

The Seer gets through two more beers before she returns her attention to me. "A deaf thang thing sword fang." Her words fall over each other on the way out and get mixed up.

I blink. "What?"

"That's the answer to your question. You said I owed you a question, and that's the answer."

"But I haven't even asked it yet."

She tries to tap her temple knowingly but misses and swipes her eye instead. "I know things. You were akssin...asking how to kill the demon, and the answer is with a Death Fang sword. There's only one of them, the death thing." She hiccups.

"What is it?"

"An inferno hell sword thingy forged in the stinky hell pits at the dawn of time. Or half past dawn. Yesh, half past dawn, that sounds right."

Now we're getting somewhere. "Where do I find it?" "

Her eyes lose focus, and she starts humming a tune.

I clench my teeth. "How do I find the Death Fang?"

She waggles a finger at me, then places her hand on my chest and cops a bit of a feel. "A piece of the Death Fang is lodged in every demon's heart. The only way to find it is from inside a demon."

"And then I can kill it?"

She cops more of a feel, running her hand over my pec, and nods vigorously. "All of them. You can kill all of them. You can pop down to Hades and have a little slaughter fest."

I swat her hand away. "At least I know where to find it."

She shakes her head. "Yes, but I don't recommender it. Demons protect it pretty hard if you know what I mean." She stage winks like we're in on some big joke. "If you go for it, there is a ninety-nine pershent chance you'll die and only a teensy weensy chance you'll live."

It doesn't matter how slight the chance is, I have to take it. If I can't defeat the demon, Scarla will never be safe, and we will never be together. Even though she and I are fated to only have a limited time together—no longer than the span of her mortal life—I will ensure we get every minute of it.

Eventually, she will go to hells, and then I will return to heaven, but in the meantime, she's mine.

"It doesn't matter how dangerous it is," I say, scraping out my stool and standing. "I'm doing it."

The Seer's face goes all droopy. "At least you'll make a pretty corpse."

I narrow my eyes. "Can't you see if I'll die?"

She pouts. "Some futures are hazy. Haaaazy. That's a fun word, isn't it?"

Good enough for me. I will turn a one percent chance

of survival into one hundred percent through sheer fucking determination.

When I reach the thick ox-hide curtains, the Seer calls out. "Don't forget to pay Oryan."

I nod and hear her mumble, "He's good for it. Don't worry, man."

I push out into the midday sun and spot someone across the street that has me instantly on high alert.

Scarla

When Zaden emerges from the Howling Cat, I'm leaning against a building across the street with my arms folded over my chest for maximum pissed-off energy.

His piercing green eyes light up when he sees me, but he covers the burst of joy with a frown.

He comes straight to me, checking up and down the dingy street. "You shouldn't be here."

I fist his black shirt in both hands and pull him close, bruising my lips against his. "What in hells below do you think you're doing?" I retort. "You rescued me from those attacking angels yesterday and saw me safely back to the Rim, and then you disappeared. You told me you'd be right back, but you never came."

"It's not safe for you to be near me. The demon is coming to reclaim its blood debt, and it snacks on mortals, in case you hadn't noticed."

His black shirt is still fisted in my hands. I release him and shove him backward. "Bullshit. I am stronger than you, angel boy. I have the dyad of power, remember? All you have is a little strength and a touch of magic."

He puts his hands on his hips, taking up my entire field of vision. "I also have immortality. The demon can't kill me. It can only hurt me."

"You don't know that. You don't know anything about it. Maybe its fangs are tipped in celestial steel, you don't fucking know."

He grins wickedly, and I'm struck anew by how damn sexy this male is. His full smiling lips are distracting. How did I ever get so lucky? Still, that doesn't mean I'll let him get away with anything.

"I know one thing about them," he says, teasing me with information.

I refuse to snap at his information bait, so I just arch an eyebrow and wait him out.

His wicked smile deepens. "I know how to kill them."

My pulse bursts into life. "You do? How?"

He closes the distance between us and cages me in his arms against the wall. "First, I need some answers from you. How did you find me here?"

I grin. "You're not the only one with contacts. Bwadu told me the most respected oracle in all of Aubia operates out of this tavern, so I figured this is where you'd be." I glance at the decrepit building across the street. "I guess this place is a good cover."

"It's not a cover. She's a drunk."

I place a hand on his cheek, feeling his jaw work as he talks. "Good, so I don't have to be jealous of her?"

He growls and leans forward, his breath warming my ear. "You don't have to be jealous of anyone."

My pulse quickens. His forest-lily scent is infused with tobacco smoke, and his muscled chest and shoulder take up my entire view. I run a hand over his pectoral muscle and circle his erect nipple. "So, are you going to tell me how to kill the demon, or do I need to go and see the nice oracle myself?"

He chuckles. "I wouldn't inflict that on anyone." His dark green eyes are dancing with black smoke, showing he's slightly turned on, although you wouldn't know it from his words. "They can be killed by a sword forged in the inferno of hell, the Death Fang."

I circle his nipple firmly. "And where is the Death Fang?"

He breathes in sharply. "I'll tell you if you promise to hide in the Rim while I retrieve it."

I pinch his nipple. "Not a chance."

He glowers, and his eyes turn full black, either from lust or anger, it's hard to be sure. "You are powerful, Scar, but you are also fragile. Would you take a precious glass vase into battle?"

I shrug. "If it could torture my enemies, then shit yeah, I would. That's a stupid argument."

He growls, and the sound is menacing and primal, making my panties wet. "You will do as I say, Scarla."

I shove him away, hard. "We've been through this, Margrave. I'm a grown-ass woman, and I will make my own decisions. Period." I mean it. I refuse to go back down the path where he makes decisions out of our mutual interest—or even worse, *my* best interest—without consulting me.

He considers it for a moment, a long fucking moment, then he closes his eyes in frustration. "Fine. You can come with me. But I want you to stay out of the way."

I can see what this costs him, that he wants nothing more than to keep me away from the demon so it doesn't suck my soul out, and I'm on board with that, I really am. But I can't stand by and let him face the demon alone, not when so much power resides in my veins.

"So where do we get this sword thing?"

Zaden looks up and down the street, though nobody is out in the midday sun. "First, we need to get as far away from here as possible."

Zaden scoops me into his arms as though I'm a child and not one of the largest and strongest women in Solren, then he beats his mighty wings, and we swoop skyward.

I let out a shriek of joy. Despite the danger, despite the upcoming battle, despite the shitstorm of my life, that feeling of leaving my stomach on the ground is delightful.

Zaden flies us half an hour west of the city and lands in a barren, scraggly-brown-grass plain without a man-made structure in sight.

I find my feet and look around. "Is it here? Is the Death Fang here?" It seems an odd place to keep an infernal sword, without a single landmark around. I was expecting to fly to a volcano or something.

He grinds his jaw. "It will be."

"What the fuck does that mean?"

"A shard of the Death Fang lives inside every demon's heart. So when one follows me here, I must reach into its chest to retrieve the shard. That's the only way to get it."

I hold out my hands. "Wait a minute, hold on. That sounds like you have to kill a demon to get the sword which is the only thing that can kill a demon. That's not going to work. Surely even you can see the logical flaw in that."

He glowers at my insinuation of his stupidity. "I don't have to kill it. I just have to reach inside it."

"Oh, that's all right then. You can just ask it to stand still while you extract its heart."

Zaden smoothes my hair, brushing a copper strand from my cheek. "Stop shouting, Scarla. It's going to be okay."

Thank the Maker I forced him to bring me along. Last time he fought the demon, he and Lazius working together had barely been able to hold it off, and his grand plan this time was to just stick his hand down the demon's throat while it wasn't looking?

Maybe he really is an idiot. At least working together, he and I might just have a chance.

We don't have to wait long. A demon flies toward us, flapping its leathery wings. In the full light of day, it looks even more terrifying than it did back in the cave. Congealed blood mats the fur around its mouth, and its sharp fangs drip with venom. The stench almost makes me gag.

When it gets closer, I notice three shimmering spots on the ground beneath it, galloping faster than any horse. The demon lands, and when the shimmering spots get near, I see they are transparent creatures.

Zaden stands between our attackers and me. "Shit. It's brought wraith hounds."

The ghostly beasts are hard to see in the daylight, so I dial up my Gaze until they shine red and orange, like they're coated in flames. They are massive dogs with slobbering jaws and oversized heads, furless creatures with pale, leathery skin coiled with thick muscle.

I try to remember my battle training and adopt a fighting stance, although I doubt it will be of any use against these creatures.

Zaden snarls, sending a ripple of goose flesh over my skin. Thank the Maker he's on my side because he is truly terrible. He flaps his wings and rises slowly to face his enemy, but the wingless wraith hounds then focus on me and step closer.

Zaden sees what's happening and immediately drops to the

ground to draw their attention away from me, leaving an opening for the demon, who swoops down and slices Zaden's shoulder. If he hadn't ducked aside, he would've lost his head.

I don't want to test the theory of his immortality, and I don't want to wait around for a new head to grow back, if that's what happens. Besides, I'm fond of the head he has.

So I'll have to deal with these hounds somehow and leave Zaden free to battle the demon.

I channel Inflict and spear it at the three hounds at once. They whimper and fall to the ground, whining like injured puppies.

Zaden glances at me, and I nod. "Go."

He takes to the air, ducking under another swipe of the demon's claws, then he manages to jab the beast with Ashmodu.

The sun beats down harder than ever, and sweat drips down my forehead and into my eyes, making it hard to focus on the three wraiths under my control. It's taking so much energy to inflict these hell beasts, much more than it takes to torture a human, and I don't know how long I can keep it up.

The ring of steel pounds the air, and I taste the salt of sweat on my tongue. My attention is focused on the three beasts, and I can only spare a glance at Zaden. He's holding his own, ducking and weaving, but a wound has opened on his side, raining red blood onto the brown grass.

He's not making any headway, just keeping up with the weaving and lunging demon.

I didn't interfere with the battle in the cave because I hadn't wanted to inflict pain on Zaden accidentally. But if I don't do something, this battle will continue for hours, and Zaden will lose blood drop by drop until he falls. I don't even know how long I can hold these hellhounds at bay.

My concentration lapses, and the largest wraith breaks out

of my control and lunges at me. I snap my head around and refocus, and it whimpers again and falls at my feet, twitching.

My energy is draining, and Zaden is losing blood.

There is one gamble I didn't want to make, but I can see I must. First, I back away from the ghostly beasts to open up some distance between us, then with a cry of "Now!" I release the hounds and inflict pleasure on Zaden and the demon.

Zaden is expecting it and doesn't falter, but the demon loses focus and stares at me.

The wraith hounds, released from their torment, scramble to their feet and gallop toward me in ghostly silence.

I need to hold the demon's pleasure for as long as I can, and I can't cast both pleasure and pain at once, so when the largest, nearest hound is at my feet, I douse it in pleasure, and it stops short, tilting its head at me in curiosity.

The other wraiths are still free, pounding toward me across the plain and kicking up tufts of grass beneath their claws.

Zaden only has a moment, and that's all he needs. He cuts open the demon's chest with his sword, reaches in with his other hand, and pulls out a shard of metal that resides where the demon's heart should be.

In Zaden's hand, the metal shard grows into a long sword dancing in red and orange flames and smelling of sulfurous brimstone.

Zaden plunges the Death Fang into the demon's unfocused eyes, and the creature disintegrates into stinking black ash that patters onto the grass.

The two galloping hellhounds stop instantly. They whine at their master's demise, then turn and flee across the plain, disappearing into daylight.

But the third wraith, the biggest and strongest of the three, remains at my feet, looking up at me with its head cocked like a curious labrador.

I reduce the intensity of pleasure I'm inflicting on the beast, but it doesn't lunge or attack. It opens its humongous mouth and pants.

Keeping a trickle of pleasure coursing through the dog, I pet its head. It nuzzles into my hand, its leathery skin softer than I expected—I wasn't even sure if I'd be able to feel it.

He's panting hard. "Are you thirsty, boy?" I look up at Zaden. "Do you have any water on you?"

He glances between me and the hell wraith. "You're kidding, right? You want to nourish the creature from the pits of hell who just tried to kill you?"

The dog whimpers slightly at that description and nuzzles harder into my hand. I take a leap of faith and remove the last tendril of pleasure I'm inflicting, tensing for an attack. But he keeps nuzzling, clearly liking the affection.

"He didn't want to hurt us, he was forced to by that demon. Isn't that right, Smokey?"

Smokey the hellhound pants happily.

Zaden sighs. "You can't name it."

I run my hand down his giant head and along his firm, muscled body. "I just did." When I reach the spot above his tail, the hellhound arches into the rub, encouraging me to scratch harder. "You're a good puppy, aren't you," I croon.

Zaden comes closer, and Smokey bears his teeth and growls, so Zaden holds the Death Fang above his head in striking position.

I stand between Zaden and the hound, protecting the dog. "Don't you dare hurt him! Put that thing away right now."

Zaden smolders. "He was about to rip my head off."

"He was just protecting me, weren't you, Smokey?"

The ghostly hound licks my leg in confirmation. I spin to face him. "Zaden is my friend, okay. He is allowed to come close, and you mustn't hurt him. Promise?"

The dog tucks his tail between his legs and looks to the grass, suitably chastened. "Good boy," I say.

Zaden sighs heavily. "It is a creature from hells below, Scarla. You can't keep it. It's not your pet. And it doesn't understand what you're saying."

Honestly, I don't know what the fuck I'm doing, but I seem to have accidentally tamed this wild beast, so I can't let Zaden kill it. "Good boy," I say, stroking the hound's head again. "You can go now."

The creature stays at my feet, panting. "You really are thirsty, aren't you, boy?"

Zaden growls behind me, snagging my attention. "What about me? I'm bleeding over here, and you're petting the creature that did it."

My sulky angel is several steps away. I close the distance and reach out to pat him on the shoulder. "You're a good boy, too," I say gently. "And we'll get you some water as soon as we can, okay?"

He snakes a hand around my waist and yanks me close against him, ignoring the low warning growl from the hellhound. "I'm not your pet either, Scarla, and don't you forget it." He kisses me hard, claiming me.

I wrap my arms around his neck, pulling him close. "Well, you kind of are. You're my pet angel."

His eyes darken. "Tell me I'm yours."

I squeeze the back of his neck. "You're mine."

"That's right." He pulls me tighter against him. "And you're mine."

"You were amazing today. I honestly didn't think it was possible to get the Death Fang, but you did it."

He kisses me, more gently this time. "I couldn't have done it without you."

I smile smugly. "I know."

He chuckles, and every line of his body relaxes. The battle tension fades from our limbs, and after a few minutes, Zaden's wound closes enough that he can fly us home. Smokey gallops over the ground beneath us, fast enough to keep up. It would be terrifying if he wasn't so cute.

I lose sight of Smokey we reach the outskirts of Solren, and I presume he's gone back to hells below or wherever he lives. Hopefully he's safe and won't get in trouble from the demons.

Thank the Maker that Zaden made it through the battle. He has the Death Fang now, which gives him a path forward. It protects him against demons and, most importantly, makes him comfortable staying by my side.

"I'll kill all the demons for you, Scarla," he mumbles as we land inside the sealed section and walk the last few blocks toward the Rim.

I believe him.

Scarla

There is nothing like a battle with a demon and a trio of hellhounds to make you appreciate a good meal.

Bwadu and her crew smuggle goods—and people—into and out of Solren's sealed section so they have access to some of the best food around. I gobble down some juicy chicken and creamy mattroot until I can't fit another thing in.

I plunk on the squishiest sofa beside Zaden and snuggle against him. My forehead scrapes against his three-day growth, and he rests a casually possessive hand down my back. We're several floors below ground, so the temperature is comfortable, but the blazing fire we are grouped around adds a lot of atmosphere.

Bwadu and her wife, Alia, sit on another couch, close to each other but not exactly snuggling. Clearly, the general is not as open to public affection as I am.

Mahari is here too. I'm fascinated by how the two sisters interact, the way they only need to speak a few words to each other to convey a complex idea, as though they share genetics and brain waves.

A scuffle near the entrance from the winding hallways that lead outside draws everybody's attention.

"Why in hells below did you bring him here? He should be in

the cells."

Two guards are disagreeing, and it's only when one shoves the other that I see the source of their quarrel. A red-haired man with his narrow lips curved in a goofy grin. My childhood best friend, Leo.

I can't help the traitorous pang of fondness at seeing him; it's like settling into a warm bath or listening to a favorite story. Despite the betrayal, despite the difficulties, his familiarity is comforting.

It doesn't mean I forgive him.

I watch in fascination as Leo sends a snaking tendril of his bruised-yellow-green vestigial power to the second guard, bringing him under his spell. Leo has Coerce, the mirror to Charm. Instead of Charm's fresh-green hue, Coerce's glow makes Leo look sickly. He can wield it to convince others to follow him, even against their own will and when the outcome is bad for them. He glows dimly, so his power is relatively weak but is still enough to be very convincing. Especially when the target has no idea it's happening.

"I just want to talk with Scar," Leo says to the angry guard, lacing his words with Coerce. It's fascinating to see my childhood friend as a man, tall and muscled, instead of the lanky kid I still think of him as.

The guard stops fighting his colleague and looks at Leo, suddenly unsure. "Fine," he says reluctantly under the magic's influence. "I suppose that's fine."

Bwadu is on her feet, striding to Leo and pointing at the door. "Take this scum to the cells immediately."

Last time she saw Leo was in VanDyke's castle when she was a prisoner, and he was her captor. No wonder she has hard feelings.

Leo turns his Coerce on her, the sickly green-yellow snake of magic winding around her, and says, "I just need five minutes with Scar. That isn't too much to ask, is it?"

I am immune to his Coerce. Unlike everybody else, I can see it and therefore protect myself.

I am curious to see how it will affect Bwadu. My theory is that she is particularly strong-willed and can resist his weak vestigial power, but I can't be sure.

She lowers her hand and stutters but eventually says. "N-no, you need to leave."

I grin. I always knew Bwadu was a formidable warrior.

Zaden is squeezing my thigh so hard he'll leave a bruise, and I have to gently prize his fingers off before I can stand up. "What do you want to say, Leo?"

Relief crosses Leo's face. I know his features so well and have spent many long hours chatting with him, exploring the forbidden North Undercity, sneaking into kitchen hubs and laughing about our pranks. Every expression that crosses his face is familiar to me, and it hurts. His betrayal fucking hurts. Even after all these months.

He smiles at me tentatively. "I came to warn you."

I sigh. I'm glad he's not opening with some lame apology that I would have to dismiss, even though part of me wants him to prostrate himself on the stone floor and grovel.

"Warn me about what?"

"The angels are looking for your hideout, and they're not far away. You have to believe me." He makes the mistake of lacing that last part with a curl of Coerce. Out of curiosity, I let the magic enter my mind and note the temptation to believe every word he says, but I'm strong enough to shut it down.

"Don't you dare use your power on me," I snarl and flick him with Inflict.

He groans and clutches his stomach. "Sorry, that was stupid."

I nod. "Like so many other things you've done recently."

"Yes," he admits. "That's fair."

Zaden gets to his feet beside me, his voice dangerously quiet, black smoke swirling in his eyes. "What makes you think we will ever believe a word out of your mouth. You've chosen your side, Leo. Now you are stuck with it."

Leo glances at Zaden but addresses me. "I've always been consistent. All I want is a better life for the people who live in the Undercity, just like we always dreamed of. That's behind everything I ever did. VanDyke promised to make me the leader of the Undercity so I could make things better for everyone. Better for you."

"Bullshit," Zaden spits. "You never wanted what was best for her. You kidnapped her, for fuck's sake."

I look up at Zaden, his stubbled jaw grinding and his eyes completely black.

I place a calming hand on his forearm. "You kidnapped me, too," I say softly.

Zaden's jaw ticks, but he stays out of the conversation, which is precisely what I want. This is about Leo and me.

Leo smiles smugly at me taking down Zaden and goes for a jovial tone that falls flat. "I mean, who hasn't kidnapped Scar, right?" The room is still, dozens of warriors watching in silence as Leo digs himself farther into his hole. "She's just so nabbable."

Part of me wants to laugh with him. That expression on his face is so familiar, the half-joke that he knows was no good. But he hasn't earned that easy friendship.

"How long do we have until VanDyke gets here?"

Leo's deep brown eyes pierce mine. "A day at most. You need to get out of here."

This is Bwadu's territory, and she commands most people around us. Mahari's warriors have been placed in homes around the city, and I'm sure Bwadu has more places we can go if necessary. But first, we need to figure out if it's necessary.

Bwadu's posture is imposing, her legs wide and her arms loose at her sides, ready for a fight. "How did you find us?" she demands.

Leo shifts his weight. "VanDyke knows Scar's in the vicinity. He's mentioned it a bunch of times. She has been spotted several times near here, and he has angels and guards looking everywhere up top." He swivels his gaze to me. "But I'm from the Undercity, same as you, so I knew you'd be underground. It's where you belong."

Zaden bristles at that comment but stays quiet.

Whenever Leo tells a lie, his eyebrow twitches. He's done it since we were kids, and it's a foolproof way to tell if he's fibbing. His eyebrow doesn't move, so I know he believes what he's saying. I look at Bwadu. "We need to leave. He's telling the truth."

The general nods at one of her top men, who snaps his fingers, and the room buzzes with movement.

The preparations are immediate. They've clearly rehearsed and prepared, running some drills because everybody knows exactly where to go and what to do. Somebody is boxing up the perishable food, others are bringing out weapons and ammunition, and others are building barricades and fortifications strategically.

Leo wanders closer, weaving through the darting people. "I

just want what's best for you, Scar," he says earnestly.

Zaden squeezes my hand. "*I* want what's best for her," he corrects.

Leo relinquishes my gaze and looks up at Zaden with his boyish grin. "Then I guess we have something in common."

Scarla

Leo is walking a fine line between the angels and the resistance.

He's still living in VanDyke's palace and acting as the angel's dogsbody, but he's bringing information on the angels' battle preparations.

There's no chance of avoiding war. We are preparing, and so are the angels.

Leo's information seems accurate. He was right about the angels invading Bwadu's headquarters within the Rim, and without his intel, many resistance fighters would have lost their lives.

He tells us VanDyke's second-in-command is Marlon, and the other top brass is Wutan. Marlon was the angel who confronted me in the streets when I was surrounded. I don't recognize the other name, but it strikes a chord in Zaden, who simmers quietly.

Leo's weak Coerce is enough to keep him safe from VanDyke, or so I tell myself. He can shrug off suspicion and redirect the angel's focus.

But if Count VanDyke gets wind of Leo's power, his vengeance will be brutal.

I can't help but worry for Leo. He broke my trust and broke our friendship, but he's still my best friend from childhood. My only friend from childhood.

Zaden thrusts at me with a bamboo sword, kicking up dust underfoot. "Why so sad, mortal?"

We are in a bricked backyard practicing our skills, ensuring we are battle ready. The space is small and dusty, protected on three sides by tall walls giving perfect privacy. A pile of garbage is in the corner, filling my nostrils with a stench. The clashing of steel against steel rings through in the courtyard. Lazius's wind-like giggle floats as he scrambles and spins around me, joining the fight.

Zaden, Lazius, and I get our combat training in while the sun is still up, leaving the precious dusk period for other warriors to practice.

This small space, and the cottage it is attached to, belongs to an elderly woman, Fra Lucerne, who lives just outside the sealed section. She is wealthy enough to afford a freestanding house with temperature resistance, but she still supports our cause. The woman stands in the cottage's upper window, watching us through the sorcered glass with a soft smile, her face creased with worry. She is risking her life by letting us stay here.

I lick my lips at the dust in the air, considering Zaden's question. "I'm worried about Leo."

Zaden scowls and aims a jab at my thigh. "That insect deserves everything he gets."

I parry his thrust and dance aside. "That insect is my best friend."

Zaden lunges and tosses my sword aside with a flick of his wrist, proving his superior skills. "Your ex-best friend. Don't forget what he did to you."

It's irritating how easily the angels can best me. It makes me fear how the upcoming battle will play out. With Gaze, I can sense movement before it happens, seeing a sparkle along the ribbon of bright light through my opponent's spine. It makes me one of the best human fighters we have. But I'm nothing against an angel who's really trying.

Lazius springs into the mix and locks swords with Zaden. "We're all on the same side now," he says. Since when did Lazius become the voice of reason? The drunken layabout I first met is nowhere to be seen. He wears a white shirt and tan trousers, and his blond-white braids flick as he dances around the yard. He looks like a warrior. A leader.

I pick up my sword from the ground and watch them spar. They move with grace and skill, their swords clashing together in a symphony of bamboo, Zaden a black blur and Lazius a white swirl.

"You don't understand, Zaden," I say, shaking my head. "Leo did what he did because he had no choice. He's trying to help us."

Zaden scoffs. "Help us? He's a traitor. He's working for VanDyke."

"He's feeding us information," I argue. "Without him, we wouldn't know half of what we do now. Like that VanDyke's second-in-command is Marlon, and Wutan isn't far behind. They're the three angels we need to worry about. Leo's risking his life for us."

Lazius joins in. "I agree with gigantor. We should be grateful that we have someone on the inside."

Zaden shakes his head. "I don't trust him. He could be leading us into a trap."

I sigh. There's no convincing Zaden otherwise. He's a stubborn ass.

Only a handful of warriors fit in Fra Lucerne's home. Me and the angels, plus Bwadu and Mahari and their top generals. This is the perfect location for our new headquarters because it is mere steps from an underground tunnel that burrows into the sealed section and pops up close to VanDyke's palace. Close to the angels but outside their home turf.

Altogether, we have almost two thousand human warriors from Solren and Desert's Maw, plus a few from rural areas of Aubia. They are housed in scattered locations throughout Solren. Lazius visits as many as he can daily and reports high morale and growing anticipation. That angel is a better leader than I will ever be...perhaps it would be better if he had the dyad, and I could go back to a simple life in the Undercity.

Watching the two angels spar, I can't stop thinking about how easily Zaden disarmed me when I pissed him off. My bamboo sword flew across the yard with a flick of his wrist. How will our warriors fare against a troop of vengeful celestials?

Their steel blades cannot kill an angel even if they strike true. Only celestial blades forged in the Maker's fires can do that.

I donated my most treasured possession, the celestial-tipped dagger that Zaden gifted me, to be broken apart into shards to be fitted at the end of our best fighters' swords.

It made twenty. Twenty warriors among two thousand will wield a weapon capable of harming an angel. The others are all pawns doomed for slaughter.

I return my bamboo sword to the holder near the big pile of trash, holding my nose when I get close. "We don't have enough celestial blades to win this war," I yell over the clashing of the angels' weapons.

Zaden is still pounding out his jealousy and fury, but Lazius stops to look at me, earning a blow to the side of his face. "Ow," he says, scowling at Zaden, then turns to me. "I was thinking about that too."

"You were?"

He rubs his temple, wiping a smear of dirt into his white-blond hair. "Yeah. So I gave my sword to the blacksmiths to break apart. They can turn it into a hundred shards or more, which will do more good than a single blade in my hands."

Zaden stops and places his bamboo sword point to the ground. He stares at Lazius, his mouth open. "What in hells below? You can't give up your Maker-given weapon."

Lazius shrugs and raises his hands. "Well, I did. I haven't used that puppy in years...I had a Hades of a time finding it, digging around in my storage bunker. Honestly, I'm happier without it."

Zaden remains a statue. "I..."

It's the first time I've seen him lost for words. He wants to help my battle—it's his battle now, too. But he can't give up his last link to heaven, Ashmodu, and I don't expect him to.

I step forward and place a hand on Lazius's arm. "Thank you. That means everything." That gives us hundred-and-twenty decent weapons among two thousand warriors, and it still isn't enough. But it gives us a chance.

Lazius has an intense look in his eyes that I'm beginning to associate with his serious side. "I meant it when I said I don't expect my warriors to give up more than me. I can't let them enter a fight without proper weapons if I have one myself. That is shit leadership, and I refuse to be shit."

Lazius looks at Zaden. "If you donate Ashmodu, we'll have enough celestial shards to arm two-hundred warriors. They could fight in groups of ten, each rallying around a single shard. We could win this war."

Zaden is pale, ashen, silent, breathing shallowly. "I can't."

Disappointment lines Lazius's face, his lips pursed and his blank gaze locked on Zaden's. But I understand my angel's decision. Ashmodu is his last link to heaven.

I square my shoulders. "We will win the battle anyway. We have to."

The sun hits the high brick walls, lowering and illuminating the courtyard in its final rays. Dusk isn't far away.

"Time to head inside." I lead the way, and the angels return their swords to the trash-hidden holder then follow me. At dawn and dusk, the courtyard belongs to the other humans, and their outdoor training sessions are crucial. We cannot steal a second of it for ourselves.

I push open the heavy door, and the temperature immediately drops. Fra Lucerne is wealthy enough to have sorcered stones insulating her cottage, which is also well furnished. The house is constructed of clay brick and stone, a two-story affair with a spiral staircase in the middle leading to the second floor. The inside is painted the color of newly fallen snow and swimming with the fragrance of freshly-baked bread.

I pull off my thick ox-hide boots and leave them near the door. The rugs are soft on my toes, and the spiral staircase creaks with the weight of a dozen footsteps as Bwadu, Mahari, and their generals come downstairs and head outside to train.

A knock sounds on the door, and Zaden opens it. "You," he snarls.

Leo pushes past and into the room, his red hair glowing brightly in the dim room. I run across and pull him into a hug. "You made it!" It's the first purely positive emotion I've felt for him in months, and it feels glorious. One moment without the complicated mix of past betrayals and broken trust. It's just so good to see him safe.

"Of course, Scar. I told you I would." The trust between us is slowly rebuilding, but it will take time.

Zaden crosses to me and snakes a possessive arm around my waist. "Your word means shit, insect."

Leo flashes a sardonic grin at the angel. "I guess that's something else we have in common. That and us wanting to take care of Scar."

I intervene before this descends into an outright shouting match. "You have to get back before dusk's end, so we'd better be quick, Leo. Do you have any news for us? Any more intel on the angels' plans?"

Leo crosses to the brown sofa and sits down, then pats the cushion beside me. "Actually, I have plenty of time. Come join me, Scar."

Zaden growls menacingly. He tows me to the couch and pulls me onto his lap. "You don't have time. You have to return to your puppet master, VanDyke, so he can tell you you've been a good little boy."

I slap Zaden's hands away and get to my feet. Nobody treats me like a ragdoll, and I refuse to be a pawn in their dick-swinging contest. "What's going on, Leo? What are you talking about?"

My old friend grins mischievously, his brown eyes lighting up. "I stole VanDyke's sword."

Lazius spins around from where he's pottering in the kitchen. "Jonshu? You took Jonshu?"

"Yep!"

"Well, fuck-the-Maker, that's perfect!"

Leo grins and accepts a hug and a back-pat from the golden-haired angel. Zaden just growls louder, hating this new development.

Jonshu, VanDyke's legendary weapon, is one of the most powerful blades ever crafted by angelic hands. With Jonshu in our possession, we have a weapon capable of destroying even the strongest angel. We can break it into a hundred shards and arm a hundred warriors.

But Zaden is not happy. His hands are balled into fists, and his eyes are fixed on Leo, his expression darkening by the second. "You stole a Maker-given weapon? You fool! Do you have any idea what kind of punishment you've just brought upon yourself?"

Leo smirks at him. "Of course I do. That's why I can't go back to VanDyke's palace. I'm officially Team Resistance now."

Zaden's eyes are black, anger simmering beneath the surface, his shoulders tense. "Great," he mutters, but I can see the cogs turning in his head. He knows as well as I do that this could be our ticket to victory.

Leo shrugs nonchalantly. "It's worth the risk if it means helping you guys win this war. Helping you, Scar."

I push Leo's shoulder playfully. "Maybe I don't hate you anymore."

Leo grins, and Zaden growls. He needs to grow up and realize how Maker-be-damned good this development is. And I have to admit, it feels fucking good to have both Leo and Zaden on my side.

Zaden

Return to where it began. That was the drunken Seer's advice, for what it's worth. So I'm here, at the Needle.

The Needle is a tall, pointed tower on a desolate rock in the middle of the ocean.

The rocky island is small, a jutting rock that belongs underwater and is constantly lashed by waves. They break with such force that the spray is hard to see through, and it stinks of fish, salt, and death.

No gulls are cawing, no crabs scurrying across the beach. Just the wind, the waves, and the narrow building stabbing the sky.

The Needle is tall, black and smooth, like obsidian. Its tip is sheared off at a sharp angle, jagged. Its top is marred by two small holes that look like eyes.

I imagine Elanora looking out those holes, staring across the roiling sea, and my jaw grinds.

The wind coming off the cold salt sea flaps my shirt until I set foot inside the only door, a small opening at the Needle's base.

I've never been inside before, though I've spent hours imagining it. It is small, dark, claustrophobic. A stone staircase is the only furnishing. It winds in a tight coil up the tower, ending at those tiny holes that look out over the ocean.

Elanora spent her life here. I dig my fingernails into my palms hard enough to draw blood—I've earned it.

Suddenly Elanora's face floats before me. Her long dark hair and almond eyes don't spark a light inside me like they once did, just guilt. The heavy mantle of guilt.

"Zaden, the Margrave of Malanox, come to visit at last," she says, her voice a ghostly howl. "I have been waiting a long time for you."

I wait for the pang of remorse that I waited so long to visit, that I could have come earlier and reunited with her. But it doesn't come. I feel oddly detached from her raw emotion. "Why have you waited? What do you want to tell me?"

"You cursed me, Zaden. I spent years of torture in this tower, and it was all your fault."

The Needle is no worse than I imagined. Heaven punished Elanora for stealing the Ring of Roth, and they could have made it worse. She had air, she had food, she had shelter.

I look into her face. So familiar, yet the longer I look, the harder it is to recognize. Did I really ever love this woman? Or do I just feel guilty for the way her life turned out?

Scarla's words pour out of my mouth. "You're a grown-ass woman, Elanora. You need to take responsibility for your own actions. I didn't ask you to steal the Ring, you just fucking took it. And you condemned me to life on earth."

My burden of guilt evaporates as I speak. Scarla has been telling me for so long that I can't make decisions for her or take responsibility for the ones she makes, insisting that she's her own person. Well, she's right, and the same applies to Elanora.

Her ghostly face twists. "That was the plan. I wanted you to stay with me on earth forever."

My remorse spirals into pity as I watch the brown eyes of the woman who's haunted my dreams narrow with anger. "That wasn't your decision to make, Elanora. I belong in heaven."

Even as I say the words, I know they aren't true. I belong with Scarla. Wherever she is, I must be. I never belonged with Elanora in the same way. My feelings for her were like water compared to the nectar of my love for the Cloaked Queen.

Elanora's brown eyes narrow, turning her whole ghostly face terrifying. "But I love you, Zaden. I did it so we could be together. Don't you love me too?"

I spent five centuries wallowing in despair, sitting in guilt at how Elanora's life ended, mistaking it for love. But it never was, and my feelings for this ragged ghost are no more than pity.

"I don't love you," I tell her gently. "But thank you for stealing the Ring. If you hadn't, I wouldn't have stayed on earth, and I would never have met Scarla."

She isn't surprised. No flicker of emotion crosses her face, and even the desperate love that twisted her features disappears. "Then what do you want from me, Zaden?" Her voice is hollow, lifeless.

"I want you to move on, Elanora. You don't belong here anymore. Your soul needs to find peace."

She nods slowly, and for a moment, I see a glimmer of gratitude in her eyes. "This is for you, Zaden."

She holds out the Ring of Roth, and as I reach to take it, she fades away, leaving behind only the sound of the waves crashing against the rocky shore. The ring tumbles to the stone floor, and I bend to retrieve it.

The ring's gold is tarnished from the centuries since Elanora stole it. I place it on my finger, and it fits perfectly, as though I've always worn it. The red gem at its center glistens like a drop of blood against my pale skin.

I stand there momentarily, taking in the emptiness of the tower. Strange to think I've spent so long fixating on Elanora and all the guilt and regret that comes with her, only to realize it was never love.

I climb the stairs to the top of the tower and look out the tiny windows at the endless expanse of the ocean. The wind whips around me, but I feel a sense of calm.

A black shape is flying through the wind like an arrow, coming straight for the Needle. It grows larger, and I can make out its black wings, matted fur, and the wicked gleam in its red eyes. A demon.

It flies to the window and reaches through with its razor claws, scratching for my face. It claws through the window, seeking a way in, seeking to hurt me, but I'm not afraid. As I watch it, a tingle of power flows from the Death Fang at my hip.

Is this what Scarla feels when she channels Inflict? The knowledge that she can protect herself and those around her? The butterflies in my stomach grow quiet and are replaced by an electric charge of determination.

I back away from the window and pull the Death Fang from its scabbard with a ring of steel. I leap from the tower window and take flight, my wings catching the wild wind.

The demon snarls in delight and launches at me, its savage claws and sharp teeth aimed at my throat.

I dart to the right, narrowly avoiding the demon's claws. The wind whips my hair, and the demon's hot breath coats the back of my neck. I spin around, swinging the Death Fang in a wide arc and slicing through the demon's flesh.

It howls in pain and lunges at me again, but I'm ready. I dodge its attack, twisting mid-air and slashing out with the Death

Fang. The blade bites deep into the demon's side, and black blood sprays across the sky.

The demon shrieks and staggers back, its eyes glowing with fury. It spreads its wings and dives at me, claws extended.

I meet its attack head-on, my wings beating fiercely to keep me aloft in the battering wind. The demon and I collide, our weapons clashing in a shower of sparks. We circle each other, each looking for an opening.

The demon charges again, but this time, I'm ready. I meet its attack head-on, my sword slicing through its flesh easily. The monster screams in agony as it falls to the rocky ground with a heavy thud, writhing in pain.

I drop beside it, my sword at the ready. "This is for Scarla," I say, my voice low and menacing, and raise the Death Fang above my head.

The demon snarls and lunges again, but I'm too fast. I dodge its attack and slice through its neck with a swift, clean stroke. The demon's head falls to the ground, and its body crumples in a heap.

I stand there, panting, my heart pounding in my chest. I wait for the demon to revive, to spring back to life and attack again, but it doesn't. The Death Fang has done its job.

I wipe the blade clean of the rotting black blood and return it to the scabbard beside Ashmodu. The red gemstone on the Ring of Roth sparkles on my finger, and when I take to the air to fly home to Scarla, my heart is light.

Zaden

I run to Scarla and find her training behind the cottage, sword in hand, barely visible in the fading light of night. The burden of guilt I've carried for so long has gone. I am at peace with Elanora's death and my role in it.

"Scar." My voice is urgent and throaty.

She turns to me and watches me approach, her face curious and questioning. The sun brings her copper hair to life, and "Where have you been?"

"I found the Ring of Roth."

Her reaction is immediate, anger rising from her in waves. "Without me? You could have been hurt!"

I grin and snake an arm around her waist, pulling her against my chest. She is yielding but strong, supple but firm. "I'm immortal, remember?"

She wriggles against me, but I don't release my grip. My cock hardens as she moves against me, and I press a kiss to her lips.

She falls into my kiss like a bottomless lake, sucking and drinking, thirsty for me. She knows what this means. "You really found the Ring?"

"Uh-huh."

"So you can go back to heaven?" There's something in her voice I don't understand, a hesitancy. She looks like she wants to tell me something, to confess some secret, but I give her a few moments, and she doesn't say anything.

"Technically. But I'm not going anywhere without you."

Her brow smooths, and she relaxes, leaning against me. Her belly pushes against my throbbing cock, and my hands run up and down her back, over the curve of her ass, around her strong shoulders.

Her eyes grow hooded and lusty. It's been days of painful separation since we were together. I thought I wanted to hold her in my arms forever, but now I'm with her, I need to fuck her.

She unbuttons my shirt and throws it to the ground. "You'd better not be going anywhere without me," she whispers throatily, her lips inches from mine.

My hands travel down her back, and I whisper into her ear. "I'm not leaving your side ever again." I press my body against hers and feel the heat radiating off her skin. She moves against me in a graceful dance, almost like we're one person, connected at the deepest level imaginable.

Our tongues tease each other's mouths as we explore each other with our hands. Her breath quickens as I caress her curves, exploring every inch of her body until she moans softly, a sweet and urgent utterance.

Snow begins to fall in thick lazy flakes. The sky is deep navy blue, and stars sparkle through the night, but I can only focus on Scarla as she stands before me, her skin glowing in the moonlight.

I slowly undress her, my hands shaking with anticipation as each piece of clothing falls away. Her curves emerge even more beautiful than I remember, her breasts begging for my touch. She stands before me, wearing nothing but the snowflakes that have landed on her skin like diamonds against velvet. My cock pulses with desire as I splay my fingers against her lower back and pull her close.

She takes my face between her hands and pulls me to her lips, our tongues intertwining passionately as we sink into one another's embrace. Icy snow lands on my face and melts in rivulets down my hot skin as we kiss.

My breathing quickens, and our bodies press closer together until no space is left between us.

I scoop up a handful of snow and rub it over her body, the cold sensation sending shivers down her spine as I cover every inch of her. Slowly, I move to her pussy, pressing the freezing snow against her. Her body quivers at the sensation, and she gasps with pleasure as I massage her with the icy crystals.

The sight and sound of her pleasure are intoxicating, and every one of her moans heightens my desire, every exposed inch of taut gooseflesh makes me harder.

The snow melts fast against her hot pussy, faster than I expected, a reminder of how quickly our time together will pass. But that makes it more beautiful, more precious, more vital.

I slip two fingers into her wet warmth and curl them slightly, finding the pressure point that makes her arch her back and call out while snowflakes coat her copper curls.

She runs her hands down my back, urging me closer to her. I bite her neck and kiss my way down to her breasts, licking and sucking hungrily at each one until she is panting with desire. I lick and stroke her breasts with my tongue while her wetness coats my fingers and hands. Her freezing nipples warm under my hot greedy mouth, and she pushes me closer.

"Wait," she says breathlessly. She pulls away momentarily to scoop fresh snow from the ground, and she rubs it on my cock. I cry out at the cold and shiver, then relax into the delicious sensation of ice against my hot body.

This is the part where I usually demand Scarla to tell me she loves me, command her to stroke my ego.

But love doesn't work like that. I can't demand it of her or force her to fall for me. I can only worship her and let her know how I feel.

I still her hand on my cock, and she looks up in surprise.

"I love you, Scarla."

Her eyes are hooded in lust, her body gleaming under the moonlight and glistening under the falling snow. She has never looked sexier.

I lean forward to kiss her full lips, but she stops me with a firm hand on my chest, a light twist to her lips. "Aren't you going to insist I tell you the same?" she teases.

"No, my love. You're a grown-ass woman. You do and say as you please."

I expect her to laugh, but she stares up at me frankly, so vulnerable and open, her wide brown eyes filled with emotion. "I love you too, Zaden."

Fuck, this woman is sexy. I can barely resist her a moment longer. Her curves are perfect, her breasts, her hips, the gentle swell of her belly. Even her limbs are lovely, but they'd be better wrapped around me.

I pick her up, and she wraps her legs around my waist, clinging to me. I place her gently over me, then slowly lower her onto my cock, thrusting slowly until our rhythm intensifies with each other's passion.

She gasps as I enter her, eyes wide with pleasure as I fill her completely. We're surrounded by snow and darkness, but between us, a fire ignites our passion like nothing else. My mouth claims hers again, our tongues sliding together in perfect harmony as we rock into each other.

We kiss until our lips are raw and swollen, until we can hardly breathe from the intensity of our lovemaking.

She meets my every thrust, and her breasts gyrate in my face, making me harder and harder. I spare one hand to reach between us and rub her clit, catching falling snow to press the coldness against her.

She curses at the coldness and moans, riding me hard and keeping a steady rhythm.

"Come on my cock, baby," I moan.

The snow falls all around us as we move together, faster and faster, until we can no longer contain our pleasure. She cries out as she comes, throwing back her head and yelling her pleasure to the sky. The sound makes me explode inside her, our love merging in a burst of energy that leaves me trembling.

We stay there for a while, joined together as one, she still straddling me, my body shaking with pleasure and relief as I hold her up. As the warmth returns to my body, so does a sense of peace and contentment, something I've never felt before but now seems essential to who I am.

Scarla smiles down at me with a vulnerable smile. Even under the falling snowflakes, it's clear: I am at her mercy, and she is at mine.

Scarla

Zaden and Leo are at each other's throats again. When Zaden and I come down for breakfast the following day, Leo greets us with a cheeky grin that pisses Zaden off.

"Are you still here, insect?"

"Yes, thank you for asking, oh, dark overlord."

I fetch water from the snowmelt beneath the chimney and fix some porridge. "Cut it out, you two, we have work to do."

The blacksmiths have been working day and night to attach the celestial shards to regular swords, and somebody has to let the warriors know they're ready.

Zaden accepts a mug of water from me. "I'll go."

I knew he would volunteer, but he's a terrible choice. Most of the humans are terrified of him or want to murder him, and I can't risk any conflicts within our ranks before the war has even started. "No, it can't be you."

Zaden and I slept in, so it's already past dawn. Leo looks toward the door then back to me. "It'll have to wait until dusk, then I'll be happy to go."

I shake my head. "It can't wait. The warriors need the day to prepare so they can move into position during dusk. We strike at snowfall."

The bulk of the battle will occur within the sealed section, so the freeze won't be a problem. The angels won't expect an attack at night.

I chew a mouthful of porridge. "It has to be me. I'll duck around all the encampments and tell them the plan. Zaden, you and Lazius can distribute the swords to the battle positions, so they'll be waiting when the time comes."

He shakes his head. "No. I'm coming with you."

Leo scoffs. "You'll just put her in more danger. Bwadu's guys aren't very fond of angels, in case you hadn't noticed, and I imagine Mahari's are the same. If you want to protect Scar, stay away from her."

Zaden glares at Leo, radiating restrained anger, his muscles coiled. "Then you have to go with her," he says slowly, spitting it out as though he hates saying the words. "You can use your filthy Coerce to protect her."

Leo doesn't bite back, which is nice. "But how? I can't go outside."

Zaden hooks a thumb over his shoulder. "I brought a couple of sorcered suits from Malanox. You can wear one."

The sorcered suits protect the wearer from extreme temper-atures. Zaden's guards and sentries wear them back home in Malanox. Seeing Zaden and Leo working together is so lovely that my heart hums momentarily, and I forget to worry about the upcoming battle.

Leo nods, and a lock of red hair flops over his forehead. "Okay." He looks at me. "Let's do it!"

Ten minutes later, Leo has donned the suit but hasn't stopped grumbling. "I look like a Maker-be-damned Margrave-lover in this." The suit is red-and-gold and bears Malanox Castle's insignia, and Leo looks like one of his guards.

Zaden grabs the other man's hand as he leaves the cottage.

"Take care of her. If anything happens to her, I'll hold you responsible."

I stifle a groan. I'm perfectly capable of taking care of myself, and I'm more powerful than Leo by a galaxy, but I don't interrupt. It's nice to see Leo and Zaden working for a common cause rather than bickering.

To my surprise, Leo doesn't retort angrily, he just nods. "I'll take care of her."

"I'll take care of myself," I mutter on the way out, earning a grin from Leo and a kiss from Zaden.

I may be impervious to damage from the sun, but I still feel the heat. The sun hasn't reached its zenith yet, but it's sweltering, and sweat coats my skin after a few minutes of walking.

"Thanks for coming with me," I say, glancing at Leo. "But I could have gone alone, you know."

He smirks. "Of course you could. You're the most independent person I know. I used to have to beg to tag along on your adventures."

"That's not true!"

He peers out at me through the visor, his brown eyes barely visible through the thick plastic. "I didn't care. Besides, I'm happy to come along and make myself feel useful. It's a sign that maybe you forgive me...?"

I've been wondering that myself. Do I forgive him? At one stage, I thought I never could, but since then, I've done so many bad things myself it's hypocritical to keep judging him so harshly.

This suit makes him slow and cumbersome, so I have to stroll so he can keep up. I fix my Gaze on him and, despite the Margrave's suit, I can still see his vestigial glow, a bruised green that makes him look sick. It's not the pure shine of a vestigial power inherited on a deathbed of natural causes, but a mirror skill. The type that can only be obtained through murder.

The buildings are getting shabbier as we walk further from the sealed section, but not quite as rundown as the hovels in Lowtown.

I kick a loose cobblestone, and it rattles into a corrugated tin sheet covering a doorway.

Before I think about forgiveness, I have to ask the question that's burning through me. "How did you get Coerce?"

Leo's gait stutters, then he resumes his steady walk. "You never asked me about that before."

"I didn't know you had it, remember? Not until I got Gaze. Have you had Coerce your whole life?"

I hold my breath, waiting for the answer. If he was born with it, I can't trust any of our history, our friendship, because I don't know how much of it was real and how much he Coerced me.

His visor moves side to side in a slow headshake. "No, I got it over in Desert's Maw."

I release a long breath. "I thought so. You always acted cagey about how you got there and what you did there, and you acted weird when you returned. Can you tell me what really happened?"

The sun is higher in the sky now and reflects off his visor at an angle that masks his face completely, but I can hear the emotion in his voice. "I went over for Dad's trading business. Like I told you, he wanted to open trade routes across the desert. That part was true."

"And?"

His shoulders rise and fall. "Over in Desert's Maw, they have these pleasure hubs out in the open, where anybody can just walk in off the street. I saw this man laying into a woman who wouldn't pleasure him, and I lost control. I was already pissed because I'd failed at my Dad's trade negotiations, and I'd been drinking all night and was fucking wasted, and I just laid into him. Fist after fist after fist. His blood was flecking out his mouth and speckling my clothes, and I just kept going, pounding my anger at him."

"Oh, fuck. That sounds awful."

He doesn't glance my way, just studies the cobblestones at his feet and strides out even longer. "It was awful. I was awful. The girl was just screaming and crying and yelling at me, but every time I looked at her, I punched him harder because...she looked like you, Scar. I know you don't want to hear that, but she did. She had copper hair like yours, but not as curly and wild. I just snapped and killed the guy. I didn't know I'd gotten Coerce initially, but I figured it out pretty fast."

Sweat runs down my spine and pools in my lower back, and all I can think about is how I failed my friend when he needed me. He acted so strangely when he returned from Desert's Maw, and all I did was needle him to tell me about his adventures. Plus, if he ever tried to get emotional with me, I shut him down because I thought he'd caught feelings for me.

But it was so much more complicated than that, clearly.

I find my words carefully. "I'm sorry I couldn't help you process all that. And when I told you I was going to the pleasure hub in the Undercity, I just got pissed at your reaction. I didn't even ask about it. I'm sorry. I should have been a better friend."

He huffs a laugh. "Wow, it wasn't expecting an apology. More like scorn and condemnation."

I think back to my own encounter outside the pleasure hubs in Desert's Maw. I came across a man pinning a woman against a wall, not even hitting her, and I lost my shit and tortured the guy within an inch of his life.

That doesn't count all the other people I've tortured just to get my way.

"Trust me, I've done worse."

The first encampment of warriors is just around the corner, and we duck inside. We pass on the message that the shard-tipped swords are ready and the warriors should move into position at dusk. Our visit is so brief that Leo doesn't even bother to doff his suit, but he throws back the visor and reveals sweaty red hair stuck to his forehead.

I grin at my old friend, an uncomplicated smile, and he shoots back his trademark mischievous smirk.

"Hi, Leo."

"Hi, Scar."

We spend several hours walking between the soldiers' encampments and passing on our message on increasingly sore feet. It is well past midday when we are nearing the sealed section and the comfort of Fra Lucerne's cottage.

The cottage is in sight when Leo's gloved hand grips my wrist, tight. A low animalistic growl sets the hairs on the back of my neck on edge, and my heart rate picks up. I smell sulfur and the stench of rot.

I spin around slowly and am faced with a hell wraith pawing the cobblestones on the street.

The hell hound is hard to see in the daylight, which streams right through it, barely interacting with its body, but when I dial up my Gaze, it is coated in red-orange flames. Slobber flicks from its oversized jaw, and it is crouched, its muscles tense beneath its pale, leathery skin.

"Shit, shit, shit," Leo mutters, then the vast slobbering

wraith growls again and lunges at Leo.

Without thinking, I put my body between the beast and my friend, and the hound stops short of attacking me and cocks its head, letting out a slight whine.

"Smokey?" Call me racist, but I cannot tell these hellhounds apart. My guy was the biggest of the three who attacked us last time, but without others in tow for a size comparison, it's hard to know how this one measures up.

The hellhound wags its tail, and I inflict it with pleasure while I reach out and rub its head. "Good boy."

"Fuck. Me," Leo says.

I ignore my friend and focus on the puppy. "Leo's a friend too, okay? No biting."

Smokey curls into my pat and wags his tail harder, so I thrill him with pleasure as a reward.

Leo backs away, heading toward the cottage up the road. "Bad boy," he mutters. "Very bad boy. If you need me, I'll be in the cottage cleaning the shit out of my underwear."

I nuzzle the ghostly hound, who nuzzles right back. "Don't listen to him, Smokey. You're the very best of boys."

Scarla

The ribbon of light down the man's spine shimmers left a full second before he darts left, making his move easy to avoid, and I fell him with a short jab to the hip.

The guards wear an assortment of uniforms, hailing from all the different angels in Solren. They are brutal and highly-trained, well-matched to the resistance fighters.

I'm leading our main attack, hundreds of men and women fighting to overthrow the angels.

It's quieter than I expected, with only the occasional scream among swords clashing and focused grunts.

Oxen-blubber lamps cast yellow pools of light over the paving stones, adding a fatty scent to the air.

Another man lunges at me, but I dispatch him in a moment. Compared to the angels I train with, even the best human fighter is woeful.

But there's not a single angel in sight. They must be tucked away safely in their castles. Assholes.

I didn't sign up to slaughter humans. I'm here to kill VanDyke and take charge of the Cloaked Council.

The vestiges dotted among the humans glow brightly in the low light, making it easy to pick out the vibrant fresh-blyberry hue of those with Clout. They are the strongest fighters, imbued with a dash of angelic strength, so I focus on those while keeping half an eye open for any attacking swordsmen.

With a thought, I tear the ribbon of light inside the strongest Clout's spine, and he topples to the floor, lifeless.

It feels wrong. Not for some moralist shit or because it'll send me to hells below, it just feels innately evil.

The second-strongest Clout strikes a young Desert Mawker, who thuds onto the ground. It takes me more effort to squeeze the ribbon of light down his spine without tearing it, but I do it anyway. He falls to the ground unconscious, but he will wake again tomorrow.

I deal with every Clout, aiming to disable rather than kill, then work my way through the other strongest fighters, taking down the ones doing the most damage to my side.

I am distracted by a flash of dark brown hair and panther speed as Bwadu battles a wiry man who is fast and skillful. She is under pressure and losing ground, so I inflict him with pain until he stumbles, and Bwadu finishes him.

Inflict is more useful for control than on a battlefield. It isn't exactly subtle, and it is difficult to pick out individuals to drill with pain among the heaving crowd.

I could inflict the whole lot of them with pleasure and turn this into a mass orgy, but that would drain me fast, so I make do with sitting on the sidelines and incapacitating the strongest fighters.

An angel appears at the far end of the street, her bright white light tinged with yellow, glowing so intensely against the darkness of night that I can't make out her features. Her wings are out, and she hovers above the paving stones, slowly approaching the mass of fighters, who edge away from her even as they battle.

She continues closer, and the battle contracts, pushing against the edge of the sealed section.

The fighters at the back are pushed onto the Rim Road, across it, and forced toward the edge as the crowd presses in to escape the avenging angel.

A woman loses her footing and topples off the edge. The fall from the Rim Road to the unsealed city below is thirty feet or more, but it won't kill her. She'll be dead from the cold before her body shatters into shards of ice on landing.

The angel is herding the humans out of the sealed section, not caring if her own guards die along with the resistance fighters.

Lazius flies to my side, watching the yellow-winged angel get closer and closer. "We have to stop her," he yells, and I agree, I completely fucking agree, but what can we do?

I stare in her direction, realizing we've underestimated the angels' power over humans. Many fighters are armed with blades with a celestial shard at the tip and could, theoretically, kill the angel. But every single one of them is backing away from her instead. We are in her thrall.

I charge her and drill her with Inflict, so she stumbles to her knees, but before I can reach her, another angel flies down from the rooftops, clad in black armor. "Don't let the Cloaked Bitch get to Solren Square," he hisses to the yellow-winged angel.

The Cloaked Bitch? I presume that's me. I lose concentration momentarily, and the yellow-winged angel is up in the air, her wings pounding as she flies away.

What are they doing in the town square? Do they have Zaden? Why do they want to keep me away? I have to find out.

The black-armored angel takes over herding the humans out of the sealed section. Another couple of warriors topple over, their screams freezing in the air.

I try to inflict the black-armored angel with a spear of pain, but I can tell my attack is weak. Exhaustion is dragging at my limbs, and my power is weak despite the adrenaline coursing through me.

He turns, and I recognize him as Wutan, one of VanDyke's top angels. My Inflict barely affects him, so I stop, hoping my power will regenerate fast.

Wutan leers at me. "Well, aren't you a disappointment! I must admit, I was expecting more from you. I suppose I'll have to make do with winning your Inflict."

I square my shoulders and focus on his shine, looking for any shimmer indicating movement. "You'll have to kill me first."

He drops his smile. "Oh, I intend to."

He lunges at me, but a ghostly beast barrels into the angel from the side and knocks him down. They roll across the ground, black armor and silver leathery muscle, a hell wraith, hissing and growling and protecting my life.

The hellhound is easier to see at night when every light atom bounces off his fur-less silver skin. Slobber flecks the ground from the hound's massive jaws, and he growls, wrestling with the angel.

Lazius ducks into the fray, timing his movement perfectly, and plunges his shard-tipped sword, but the angel rolls aside and crouches, alert.

Lazius spares me a quick look. "I will stop him," he says. "I'll kill him, or if I can't do that, I'll lead him away. You go do what you need to do."

Can I just leave these hundreds of humans without helping save them? What if Lazius fails? Then every last one of them will be forced into the unprotected night and freeze to death.

Fuck it, I have to trust him. He's a better leader than I ever will be, with more strategy in his little finger than I have in my entire body, so if I can't trust him to pull this off, I can't trust myself.

I nod. "Do it."

Smokey comes and nuzzles me, but I can't muster any pleasure to inflict him with, so I just pat him instead. "Good boy. Thank you for saving me."

He nuzzles my hand, wags his tail, and runs his long body alongside me, pushing against me like he's trying to tell me something.

"Do you want me to ride you?"

Smokey's tail wags, which I take as a yes.

I half jump, half pull myself onto the ghost hound's back, and wriggle until I am straddling him. He is mostly transparent, so I can still see the cobblestones beneath me, but he feels cool and solid. I lie flat against his leathery body and whisper into his ear. "Let's do this."

Zaden

One of VanDyke's guards, dressed in dark leather armor with an indigo stripe running down the sleeve, attacks me with a wide unstable swing.

His sword can't really hurt me, but it's easy to swat aside anyway. Then I slice him in two with Ashmodu and step back out of the splatter zone.

That's one less man between Scarla and her throne.

My face is glamored, so the guards can't tell I'm an angel, and the fools keep attacking me. I take them down one by one but derive little pleasure from it.

Around me, a group of Bwadu's Solren warriors battles the crew of VanDyke's guards outside the Count's gold and marble palace.

Leo knows this area well. He brought us here, taking a winding path through the small forest so we could arrive unannounced.

We struck at snowfall, our goal to sneak into VanDyke's opulent monstrosity of a home and kill him as he slept.

But they were expecting us. I cut a sideways glance at Leo, who appears to be battling the guards as furiously as anyone. Could he have betrayed us? Could he have betrayed's Scarla once again? After all, he's done it before.

Another indigo-striped guard attacks me clumsily, and I disarm him then plunge Ashmodu through his chest. The little heap of bodies at my feet makes new attackers think twice, so I have a moment's reprieve.

The tang of iron in the air mingles with the scent of sweat. Groans and the ringing of steel are everywhere. Fat snowflakes drift lazily down, far fewer than outside the sealed section. They are trodden underfoot before they can layer onto the cold ground.

But VanDyke is nowhere. I hoped to end his life and end this war in one fell swoop, but the bastard must be cowering in his palace, which is protected by magical wards. The only way in is through this gate, which means getting past these guards.

Leo is losing ground in a fight against a taller man, and I wait for the right opportunity, then send a tiny spark of Angelfire at his opponent, who crashes to the ground. Leo nods gratefully at me, then turns to the next guard.

I dare not use Angelfire generously for fear of hitting our own warriors. Human life holds a meaning for me now that it never used to, thanks to Scarla. She would never forgive me if I killed Leo, accidentally or not.

I hope she's okay. She insisted on leading the main attack, the big battle in the city streets, aiming to distract the angels while we creep in to kill VanDyke.

But it hasn't worked out that way for us. I just hope her battle is going according to plan.

The only angel in sight is Marlon, VanDyke's second-in-command. His coal-dark skin absorbs the night, his dark eyes flashing as he supervises the indigo-slashed guards and keeps his own hands clean. He occasionally launches Angelfire indiscriminately into the fray, not caring if he hits his own men.

A guard sprints out of the woods along the main path, beelining for Marlon. Checking my glamor is in place, I edge closer, one eye on my swordfight with his men and the other on the angel. I need to hear what the messenger says.

The runner reaches Marlon's side, panting, not bothering to keep her voice low. "The trap for the Cloaked Bitch is set. She's headed for Solren Square."

The Cloaked Bitch? That has to mean Scarla.

Leo is beside me, his red hair plastered to his face in sweat. It may be cold and dark at night, but he fights hard and fiercely.

His brown eyes pierce mine. "Go help her. Go help Scar." I am frozen by the thought that I let Scarla go into battle without a celestial blade while I hold Ashmodu in my hands. At my moment of inaction, Leo screams. "Go!"

I can see Scarla hanging upside down by the ankles in the Solren Square, swinging back and forth from a long rope, her hands tied and her mouth bound, her magic silenced. I don't know if it's possible, but the image is so stark that I cannot breathe for a moment.

My glamor falls away, and Marlon sees me and lunges at me with his sword.

I blink, statued in panic, watching as he attacks me.

Leo dives in front of me and takes the celestial blade's blow, saving my life.

He falls to the ground, curling up on the grass like he's going to sleep, his hair stark against the green grass as snowflakes drift onto his cheeks. I don't have time to see if he's okay.

If he's not, he just sacrificed his life for Scarla's. He just sacrificed his life for mine.

I take to the skies and fly as fast as possible for the town square with Marlon on my tail. I have to warn Scarla about the trap.

I won't let Leo's sacrifice be in vain.

Scarla

Riding Smokey is smooth and fast, and the hell wraith responds to my thoughts like lightning. A gentle caress of pleasure to his left, and he turns left, winding through the streets of the sealed section like a snake.

The sounds of battle are everywhere, cries, grunts, shouts, pounding feet and screaming men, the ringing of steel against stone.

We gallop toward the battle center, where even the alleyways we blur past are filled with fighting.

Mostly, it's human guards battling human resistance fighters, so the angels are winning either way. The angels send their human minions to fight in the uprising and keep themselves safe.

Solren Square is outside the ornate grand palace where the Cloaked Council convenes. Its broad, hand-carved paving stones are where the heaviest fighting rages. Where the angels don't want me to be.

Smokey is cold between my thighs, and the salty iron of blood fills the air. A line of angels stands on the marble palace steps, watching their guards fight the warriors. Zaden is here, fighting VanDyke's second-in-command, Marlon, whom I recognize from his coal-black hair and ebony wings. Their movements are so fast their shines blur, and I have to dial back my Gaze to make out their precise forms parrying and sparring. Zaden is absorbed in the battle, his eyes black in a killing haze.

But most of the angels are out of the action, watching calmly. At their center, VanDyke stands serenely with his arms folded across his chest and his expression unreadable. He is in full cherub gear, with a golden cloak and pure white pants.

I aim to get them bloodied.

Smokey steps lazily over a fallen guard in VanDyke's indigo-slashed livery. The hell beast snaps at a second guard who jabs at me from behind and rips the poor woman's head off.

I have to stop this violence. It's too much death, and only the humans are dying while the angels look on.

"Stop!"

It's like shouting during snowfall in the middle of a field, my words muffled and silent beneath the raging of the battle.

I raise my sword and shout again, but nobody listens. I trickle Gaze and focus on the ribbon of light running down each fighter's spine. I select the nearest guards and gently squeeze the light ribbon right behind their necks, and they topple to the ground as one, thumping onto the paving stones.

The warriors look around, startled, as their opponents suddenly collapse, and their attention lands on me. But I don't have everybody's focus yet, so I reach out to the next ring of guards and make another dozen or so of the angels' men collapse, unconscious. After a third round of cutting the guards' strings like a manic puppeteer, I finally have the attention of every last creature in the square.

"Enough violence," I call in a ringing voice. "This ends here."

Angelfire shoots toward me from the stairs, spears of red, orange, and green that only I can see.

Before they reach me, a shield snaps up around me, and the celestial attacks bounce harmlessly off.

The shield is bright white, tinged with purple. I recognize that color magic—Zaden. He has left himself exposed to protect me.

I glance at the stairs where he was fighting Marlon, but he is gone. A moment later, he is at my right knee, stepping inside his own protective shield and standing at Smokey's side.

"Thanks," I murmur. "That was just in time."

He winks. "I told you you needed me."

"There was never any doubt, angel."

I have to take advantage of the battle's attention while I still have it, so I project my voice as loud as possible. "I will make you a deal, VanDyke. Fight me one-on-one, you and me. Swords only. Whoever wins is the victor, and the fighting stops."

Zaden looks up at me, his jaw going slack. "Scarla, no!"

VanDyke looks every inch the King he's itching to be. He spreads his arms wide like a benevolent leader. "You have created such a beautiful spectacle, Scarla, I would hate to deprive you of it."

I dig my hands into Smokey's cool skin. "You are losing a lot of guards, VanDyke. Wouldn't it be easier to face me by yourself?"

VanDyke smiles. I can see his perfect white teeth from here. "Humans are easy to breed, Scarla. They don't even need loving mothers, as you know."

Zaden growls, and I place a hand on his shoulder to stop him from doing something stupid. That's my job.

"But wouldn't it be satisfying to kill me by your own hand? You've been after me for Gaze, but that's a long game. If you kill me on the battlefield today, you'll get Inflict, enough to rule the Cloaked Council."

His eyes practically dance with glee while he considers my proposition. Frankly, it's a good one for him. Even against my Inflict and Gaze, he has the advantage of strength, speed, experience, and skill.

Zaden's voice is pitched quiet and comes out of a clenched jaw. "Don't do this, Scarla. You can't beat him."

I want to bite back that I've beaten *him* several times, but I know that's a lie. The only time I ever got close to besting Zaden was when he went easy on me or if I distracted him with sex. Well, maybe I can do the same with VanDyke.

The oversized Cupid descends the steps regally, slowly. "What an interesting proposition. You and I will act as champions for our own sides. And when you are killed, your colleagues agree to bow their heads to me?"

He isn't looking at me, he's staring directly at Zaden, looking for confirmation.

Please, Zaden. Trust me. I'm a grown-ass woman, remember. You have to let me make my own decisions.

Zaden doesn't wait longer than a few heartbeats before answering, his voice ringing with authority. "It is Scarla's decision, and I will stand by it." He spreads his arm wide to encompass every resistance fighter. "We will all stand by it. If you beat her, we will submit to you. But when she beats you, the angels will all bow to her as their Queen."

VanDyke chuckles, an orchestrated sound as false as my mother's love. "Marvelous. I believe we have a deal. But," he holds up a finger. "You mustn't use Inflict during the battle."

I keep my face a mask, but seriously...how the fuck am I supposed to win without Inflict? That removes my one ace in the game. But I have to stop the violence somehow, I have to stop the murder. And, sooner or later, I have to face VanDyke.

"Fine," I call.

The center of the square clears of fighters, all moving to stand in a loose ring around the edges. Several bodies are left behind, and I try to calculate how to use them to my advantage during the fight. Perhaps VanDyke will trip over one and hit his head on the pavers?

Bwadu and Mahari make it to my side during the shuffle, looking fierce.

"What the fuck do you think you're doing?" Bwadu shoves me so hard I almost fall off Smokey's back. The hell beast growls at her, and she backs away a foot but is still spitting in anger.

Zaden answers for me. "She has it under control. If she says she can beat him, she can. End of story."

I love that male. I fucking love him.

Mahari looks as furious as her sister, but I can see her taking in the blood and death around the square. Half a dozen of her warriors are lying in the open space, and I bet she knows each and every one personally. She scans the area, then locks her dark brown eyes on mine. "Can you win this fight?"

This is no time for hesitation, so I force out a sharp nod and keep my voice steady. "I can."

Mahari looks at her sister. "Then I say we do this."

VanDyke is in the center of the square. He's removed his golden cloak and is wearing pure white, like the perfect angel he isn't. "Having second thoughts?" he calls.

I don't bother answering. I just slide off Smokey's back and stamp my feet.

VanDyke goads me again. "I can't see if you're using Inflict, but I can tell. And so can Marlon." He nods toward the line of angels, one of whom has an arrow knocked in a bow aimed at my heart. "If I get hurt for no apparent reason, Marlon will release that arrow straight into your chest. I'm sure you agree that's entirely fair. Just to make sure you don't cheat."

I pull my sword from my scabbard and step toward my opponent, but Zaden grabs my wrist and pulls me to him, smelling of sweat and blood. "Cheat, Scarla," he whispers fiercely.

I give him a tight smile. "Of course."

"And don't die." He presses a bruising kiss to my lips, then releases me.

Five steps forward, and I'm in my fighting position against an angel. He never said I couldn't use Gaze, so I tune it and focus on his glow. Before every movement, the thick ribbon of light down his spine sparkles, giving me a slight advantage. He darts left, but I pick up the movement and step aside.

"Very good," he says.

"Condescending prick," I mutter and duck away from another swipe.

I gave up my celestial dagger, but a shard of it was embedded into the tip of my sword. A glancing slice won't hurt VanDyke for long, but if I can pierce his heart with my sword tip, he'll be done.

The first few parries feel like a warm-up, like I'm starting a training session with Zaden. He parries right, I duck left, he circles one way, I watch carefully and keep him at bay, matching his movements.

Then VanDyke shatters the illusion and lunges right for me, faster than I predicted. His aura shimmers the barest amount a millisecond before he lunges, just enough to save my life. I curve my back and jump backward so his blade gashes my belly rather than splitting me in half.

"That wasn't quite as good," VanDyke chides like a psychopathic mentor.

Fury hits me right before the pain, which glances across my chest where his sword sliced me open. A hand to my belly comes away red, and pain cuts through my thoughts.

But I've met pain before and conquered it. I inflict myself with a tiny dose of pleasure, just enough to take the edge off the pain but not enough to distract me.

I meet the Count's next below with a block, feeling the shudder of the contact run up my arm and make my shoulder tremble. Maker-be-damned, he's powerful.

"What a strong little human," he says. "But not quite strong enough."

He dances around me and lunges again, slicing my left arm. Count VanDyke wields a celestial blade that can kill an angel, so I won't last long even against these glancing blows.

But he doesn't have his own blade. "Not using Jonshu today, VanDyke? Oh, that's right, we stole it and broke it into pieces. A hundred shards that can never be repaired."

The angel simmers in rage, grinding his jaw. Hopefully it will make him sloppy.

I inflict a little more pleasure on myself and keep my feet firm, though my movements are already sluggish from blood loss.

I just need to get in one blow, one strike, but he's faster and stronger than I predicted.

Suddenly, I'm glowing purple-white, and for a second, I wonder if I'm dead. My glow is the exact shade of Zaden's magic, so it must be something he's doing.

I duck under a high swing from VanDyke and stumble to the

left, just managing to escape a diagonal slice.

Jonshu nicked me, I'm sure, but I don't feel a thing.

I glance over at Zaden, whose brow is knitted in extreme concentration. He is casting a shield over me, melting it around my body so VanDyke can't tell it's there.

Perhaps I have a chance after all.

VanDyke has a smug look on his stupid smug face, and while he's distracted by his own excellence, I dart in and aim a blow at his closest leg. He's faster, though, and ducks aside, tutting at me like I'm a naughty child.

I'm losing blood, but not as fast as I should be. I glance down at my belly to gauge how much longer I can last in this battle and see a sunny yellow haze, which I track back to a warrior in the crowd. A Healer.

I might have a fucking chance indeed.

With renewed energy, I dance around, jumping out of the way of most blows and meeting others with my own.

I can see VanDyke's face calculating, already mentally writing his victory speech. He doesn't have a shield up, so he's apparently abiding by the rules of our engagement. Idiot.

No more of his blows land, thanks to Zaden's protective shield, but VanDyke will notice soon, so I have to act fast.

He signals an upcoming movement with a light shimmer to the right side of his aura, and I don't dart away. I lunge into the action, meeting him, letting his sword pierce my hip and bringing my own around to slice his cheek, giving him a matching scar to the one Zaden gave him in the Undercity.

I inflict that wound with every ounce of pain I can muster, and he stumbles backward, clutching his face.

I take advantage and lunge my sword into his chest, and the celestial shard pierces his heart.

VanDyke's face is a mask of horror as he locks his dark blue eyes on mine, falls to his knees, and then pitches face onto the stone pavers.

The world is silent, and I take a few moments to watch VanDyke, following the blood seeping from his cheek and soaking into his cupid-blond curls, tracing around the pavers.

When I look up, every face in the square is on me.

Human guards crowd around the edges, and angels line the palace stairs. Lazius stands between the two groups with his sword in his hand, and Wutan stands nearby as though they've just finished fighting. Hopefully, that means he saved the humans at the Rim Road.

Lazius is the first to move. He drops to one knee and bows his head, his white-blond hair catching the lamplight. "My Queen."

Nobody expected this outcome, least of all the angels. Marlon and Wutan cast bolts of Angelfire at me, but Zaden's shield still protects me. I repay the two angels by inflicting them with agony, and they both buckle to their knees.

It is enough to encourage every other angel to go to their knees and declare me their Queen.

Some do so willingly and fast, those who never supported VanDyke. Others are slower but still submit. There will always be a few I need to keep an eye on, probably more than just Marlon and Wutan, but I will deal with them later.

I turn and lock eyes with Zaden on the far side of the square. He once told me he would never bow to me, and I don't expect him to. So when he goes to his knees and says, "My Queen," I flinch and give a tiny yelp. Very queenly.

Every human in the vicinity falls to their knees, bowing before me.

We won the war. I won the battle. I am the Cloaked Queen. And, apparently, the humans' queen.

Zaden

Leo's funeral is the next day.

Scarla's first act as Queen was to declare that every human who fell in the battle shall be buried within the sealed section, an honor rarely bestowed on even the wealthiest people.

She declared that those people would not be forgotten, that we would plant fields of flowers over their remains so their sacrifice would be remembered.

She stands beside me in her battle gear as the city elders offer a blessing to the Maker and sprinkle dirt over Leo's body. Her pants and tunic are dirty, torn in places, and I suppose she wears them to keep a connection with the fallen soldiers, holding on to what she had yesterday.

Scarla's shoulders shudder, her whole body wracked with sobs as she stares at his lifeless body in the ground. She looks smaller than usual, hunched in on herself, her vibrant hair hiding her face.

I push a lock of her hair behind her ear and put an arm around her shoulders, but I can't stop her pain.

"He died for me," I say, but she doesn't respond, just shakes harder.

Hundreds of men and women died yesterday; everybody lost someone. Mahari, Bwadu, I feel for their losses, but I can't care the way I care for Scarla. Her sadness burns through me like physical pain, and I wish I could take it away.

After the ceremony, she grips my hand tight while the people around us disperse quietly. "Tell me it was worth it."

Human lives are so fleeting, which I used to think made them worth less than mine. But perhaps I had that round the wrong way, and the very brevity of their lives is what gives them value. Like precious gems.

I cannot begin to weigh the cost of those lost lives against what we've gained, so I ask a question instead. "What are you going to do as Queen?"

Some of her old vigor returns as she lists all the changes she wants to make, the improvements to people's lives she's been dreaming of for years. Expanding the sealed section of Solren. Installing a sealed section over Malanox and other smaller towns. Improving the distribution of resources, ensuring even the poorest people have a variety of food to eat and a career choice. Adding color and joy to people's lives.

I still don't know if that makes it worth it because the longer I spend with Scarla, the more I realize how little I understand humans. I cannot weigh human happiness against human lives.

But Scarla can. Her beaming grin lights up her face, shining through the tears. "It was worth it. I would gladly have given my own life for the changes we can make, and I know Leo would too."

"He did." I was jealous of that human, of his close relationship with Scarla, but he was a good man in the end and did what he had to so I could get to Scarla's side.

The thought of her giving up her life for anything has me squeezing her hand and pulling her close, capturing her in a kiss, licking away her salty tears. "Do you trust me?"

She kisses me back. "Of course."

"Then come with me."

An hour later, I push open the rusty door of the Howling Cat. The tavern is outside the sealed section, so news spreads here slowly, but rumors abound of the battle and change of leadership, although nobody seems sure of the details.

Except for the Seer of Howlka. She greets me with a smattering of applause, and when she sees Scarla behind me, she bows. "Honored to meet you, my Queen."

Scarla shifts uncomfortably and glances between the Seer and me, so I run the introductions, including the barman, Oryan.

Oryan narrows his eyes at Scarla's dirty and torn battle clothing, then nods at the large sack I'm holding, wiggling his furry eyebrows. "What's in the bag?"

The Seer grins. "I already told you. It's your payment in full. Isn't that right, Margrave?"

I heave the sack onto the bar. "Ten years' worth of booze for your best customer."

"Plus interest," the Seer says.

"Plus interest," I agree.

Scarla looks baffled by the exchange, so I give her a quick rundown, and she smiles appreciatively at the Seer. "Well played."

The Oracle smirks. "I knew I'd like you."

I hope Scarla adds the oracle to her list of friends, which I know she keeps a mental tally of. She'll never replace Leo, but she will have to move on.

The barman slides two shots of fire whiskey across the sticky bar, and the Seer downs them both before I can stop her.

"Maker-be-damned," I grumble. "Can't you stay sober for two seconds so you can answer me straight?"

Two strings of lanky hair twist together over her face as she wobbles her head. "Nope."

Scarla snorts a tiny chuckle, more bemused than amused, but at least she's not sobbing anymore. "Did you just bring me here to meet this excellent woman?" Scarla asks, accepting her own shot of fire whiskey and downing it in one.

"No. I came to ask for her advice."

The Seer claps her hands together in glee and wriggles her ass to right herself on her stool. "Advice! That's my favorite. I get so bored of *Can you tell me the future?* And *When will I die?* And *Will I be rich?* And *Who will I marry?*. It's nice to be given free rein for change. Okay, let me see... I advise you to dress in purple, not black. It really brings out your eyes."

Scarla chuckles. "I've been telling him that for years," she slurs.

Humans have such weak tolerance for alcohol, especially fire whiskey.

"You really haven't, mortal," I tell her.

Scarla lifts a finger. "Have too."

"I haven't even known you for years."

Scarla pouts and orders another whiskey. "But in a couple of years, I'll have known you for years, and by then, I will have been telling you that for years. I'm just getting in early."

Maker-be-damned, the nonsense in this tavern seems to be contagious. The Seer nods serenely. "I told you I give excellent advice. You're welcome."

I sigh and decide to give in and order my own fire whiskey. It won't get me as drunk as the humans, but I've earned it. Better to join in than be left behind.

The liquid burns my throat and sears my stomach, sending a tingle of warmth through me. Scarla sits on a stool, and I stand behind her and drape myself over her, resting my hands on the bar. She smells of sweat, blood, and dirt, and I want to take her home, bathe her wounds, and tuck her into bed.

"That wasn't the advice I was after," I begin explaining, but the Seer cuts me off with a raised chin.

"Just let me have my moment, Margrave."

I pause a beat and then say, "One. That was your moment. Now, I need advice on how Scarla and I can be together forever. I know she's doomed for hell, but I will follow her to the pits of Hades if there is a way I can. So my question is this. How can I, an angel, get into hell?"

Scarla gives a little humph of displeasure at the question, not wanting me to spend eternity in hells below. But she doesn't object because she *does* want me to spend eternity with her.

We both look at the oracle expectantly. Her elbows are on the sticky bar; she picks one up and tries to lick it before answering. "If you want to be together forever, just go through the gate thingy in the desert."

Scarla surprises me by saying, "The gate to heaven?"

"That's the one," the Seer slurs. "I can never remember what it's called."

"But I can't go through because I've commimmered murder. Commimmered. Comrittered. Oh, you know what I mean."

The Seer gesticulates wildly. "Oh, angels can get away with anything. A smite over here, a smite over there, a spot of avenging between smites. Honestly, you guys can murder or even steal someone's drink and still get into heaven."

Disbelief crawls over Scarla's face, her brows knitting together. Her eyes wide, she turns to me, mouth parted in a question she doesn't voice. I can read her well enough to see she's losing faith in this woman, who apparently can't even *see* that Scarla isn't an angel.

The Seer waggles a cranky finger. "Don't think at me like that, I'm not an idiot. I know you're not an angel. But you have the vestigial powers of an angel, so you're exempt. You can do all that smiting and avenging too, and you don't get a blemish on your soul."

I slump so hard over Scarla's shoulders that I almost drag her off the stool. Can she still get into heaven? And I have the Ring of Roth, so I can get in too.

I lean down and murmur in her ear. "Did you say the gate of heaven is in the desert?"

She nods, smelling of excitement. "Yep, I saw it. I'm sorry I didn't tell you yet. I was going to, I just...."

I let out a whoop of joy and pick my mortal up, spinning her around and holding her close. She and I have found a way to be together beyond her fleeting lifespan.

Zaden

The next few days are eerie, with the streets of Solren teetering between wild joy and empty despair.

It takes days to bury the dead, and every second person I pass has a weight on their shoulders that speaks of grief.

But every other person is leaping for joy.

The Rim Road access has been opened, so anybody can enter the sealed section. New people arrive every dawn and dusk, walking outside during the day and the night, marveling at the sun, clouds, and stars. It is their first time outdoors during the day or night, and their wonder is boundless.

But the streets are getting crowded. They will need to solve that before it becomes a problem. I just hope Scarla doesn't decide she's the one who needs to find the solution.

The Seer told us she could go to heaven, and I'm so glad. I won't spend the rest of my endless life missing her and playing out scenes in my head of her being tortured in hells below.

But she's a pioneer at heart, always wanting to make the world better for others, so I don't know if she'll ever agree to go to heaven. At least, not until she dies of old age, and I don't think I can wait that long. But if she wants to stay here on earth, I will stay with her. I'll never leave that woman's side again.

The sister generals have moved into VanDyke's palace and

liberated all his servants, though many chose to stay. It is the new headquarters for the resistance...Or, I suppose I should say, the government. Bwadu and Mahari have a lot to figure out. I hear Mahari plans to return to Desert's Maw, and most of her people will go with her, returning to their loved ones. But plenty will stay and help rebuild Solren into a new vision of what it can be. Shared resources, a livable environment for all.

I just hope my mortal is happy to set aside her personal involvement and let others do the heavy lifting. She's earned a rest in heaven.

My feet ring on the marble floors of VanDyke's palace. I can always tell where Scarla is because her heavy ox-hide boots thud and echo. People are everywhere, teeming through the ornate halls, looking extra bedraggled among the Count's finery and opulence. The floor is an ocean of gold-veined white marble, and massive white pillars support the distant ceiling, which depicts mortals adoring a golden angel. How did I never notice how self-important that was?

Decisions must be made, laws enforced, and a whole new order must be established. I just hope my woman doesn't want to be part of it.

I'm itching to pull her aside, and I bide my time, counting the hours and days and waiting until her mourning for Leo isn't so fresh.

I find her sitting in VanDyke's extravagant library, a vast room lined with shelves of hardback books. An antique, carved desk made from real Rosen hardwood, no doubt from the Leyva forests, puts a sweet woody scent into the room. A crackling fire provides gentle background noise.

She looks up from the book on her lap, and her eyes are molten gold in the reflected firelight. The tip of her tongue is wet and pink. "Hello, sexy."

My heart melts. "Hello yourself." She is so fucking gorgeous, sitting there with the book on her lap, her wide brown eyes blinking up at me. Her copper hair graces her shoulders, flowing around her like a wild halo, her light freckles like kisses from the Maker. She is wearing a burnt orange dress that drapes her body.

"I didn't know you could read," I tease.

She whacks me on the leg as I perch on the side of her chair. "Yes you did, asshole."

I slide down the armrest until I'm squishing her, and she wriggles and groans, making me love her more. "How did you get so sexy?"

"Born that way," she shrugs.

"And how did you get so patient and clever and resourceful?"

"The patient part is from spending so many hours in your tiresome company," she jokes with a small smile. "Everything else is a natural bounty."

I lean closer to her until our noses are nearly touching. She's bathed in lily-scented water, my favorite smell in the entire world. I could inhale her. I could stay here forever.

"Are you sure you can leave Solren?" she asks.

"What do you mean?"

"You're a crusader, woman. I know part of you is itching to finish your work, to ensure everybody gets three chef-prepared meals daily and wears the finest silks."

"You're an idiot," she says affectionately.

I grin. "Why, thank you." The lightness in my heart is so welcome. After so many years of struggle, pain, and heavy guilt surrounding Elanora, I feel free. I am buoyant, as light as the clouds.

I cup her chin and stare directly into her eyes. "But, if you want to stay here, I'll stay with you."

Her expression softens at this, and she looks away momentarily before meeting my gaze again. "I can't ask you to do that. I know how badly you want to return to heaven. It's all you've ever wanted."

"That used to be true." A smile creeps up my face, and my heart beats faster. "But now all I want is you."

I pull her onto my lap, so I'm not squishing her anymore. I smooth her burnt orange dress over her legs.

She sweeps in and steals a kiss before pulling away with a playful wink and a coy grin. "You big old softie."

I let out an amused laugh. "Well, that's a new one. No one ever accused me of being soft before. Heartless? Evil? Uncaring? Sure. But never soft! You wound me."

"You have the softest, gooiest, squishiest, blyberriest heart of anyone I've ever met," she teases, and I clasp my chest in mock horror.

I kiss her then, long and slow and filled with passion. My body responds, my cock twitching beneath her leg. The taste of her is exquisite and tantalizing. I want to taste more, to explore every inch of her body.

She sighs, and I know the feeling of her body against mine is something I want to indulge in over and over and over again.

My hands wander to her thigh, feeling the smoothness of her skin beneath my fingertips. I can't get enough of it. I run my hands down her legs, tracing their curves and paying particular attention to the places that make her gasp and moan.

Her body is like a river: ever-changing, never-ending, and full of surprises. Every touch tells me something new. A muscle in her thigh tenses beneath my exploring fingers.

She pulls me up to meet her lips, our mouths melting into each other's as if they were made from the same fire. I tangle my fingers in her copper hair as she slides across my lap.

She shivers as I explore, and it's like a siren song when she moans. But we're in VanDyke's library, which is not the place for such things. So instead, I trail my fingers back down her leg before resting them on either side of her ankle.

It takes all my strength to pull away from her and break our kiss. But when I do, there is no masking the hunger in our eyes.

"I wonder what kissing you will feel like in heaven," I murmur.

She leans forward and nips my lower lip, then wiggles her ass across my cock. "It can't be any better than this."

Zaden

Whenever I see Scarla directing another warrior-turned-builder or attending another meeting about how to deal with the influx of people to the sealed section, where to house them, and how long until we can construct a larger seal, I'm proud. So fucking proud.

She's done more with her tiny lifespan than I've done in hundreds of years.

But I'm also scared. She is embedding herself more and more into life here. Whenever I sneak a glance at her, I struggle to hide my worries. Her brow furrows as she searches my face for an answer, and I can see the same haunting loneliness in her eyes that is in mine. A twinge of guilt seeps into my heart as I realize my sorrow is now hers too.

Finally, two weeks after the battle, she pulls me aside in one of the palace's courtyards, painted with scenes of ancient wars. A fountain in the courtyard's center is surrounded by lush, tall grasses and colorful flowers of every size and shape. Yellow and red buds, blue roses, drooping purple and orange blooms, and one resembling a tub of blyberries.

Scarla is dressed in dark pants and a green cloak, with a silver belt and a circlet on her upper arm. She looks more regal every day. "It's time," she declares.

Hope lifts in my chest. "Really?"

She nods, smiling. "Let's go through the gates and get you home."

I grasp her wrist, hard. "Get us both home, you mean?"

"Of course. Is there any business you need to tie up first? Like, telling the people of Malanox you're leaving."

I shake my head. "Lazius is going to take care of it for me. He has my full authority to do whatever he wants with my castle—"

"As long as—"

I cut her off with a finger. "As long as he consults all of the servants currently living there and lets them make their own choices," I finish for her, earning a hug and a grin.

I consider if there's anything I need to do before I leave. A few of the angels are in the cells below Belial's palace. Lazius confiscated their celestial swords and set a rotating watch of the more trustworthy angels to monitor them. They'll be a handful, but Lazius is a competent leader. He can handle them.

Bwadu is consulting with some rich folks and some community leaders from the outskirts about how to move forward. Everything is under control, and I'm ready to leave. Tapping my foot, I put a hand to my sword and glance at the door. My stomach flips in anticipation of the journey ahead.

"No loose ends," I confirm. "I'm ready to leave at your word."

She looks at me with a smirk. "Word."

I pick her up and spin her around, breathing in the faint blyberry smell that never left her. I want to leave immediately and march right out the door, but Scarla insists on having one last dinner with our friends.

She also insists that we don't tell them our plan to leave. "It'll ruin the vibe," she tells me. "I don't want my last night with them to be sad. Let's keep it light and happy and leave on a high note." I'm happy to follow her lead, so we keep our intended departure quiet.

She appears for dinner wearing dark brown pants that hug her hips and a deep-necked green shirt that exposes the tops of her delicious white breasts. All evening, I glance down at her cleavage and remind myself that dinner is to say goodbye to our friends, not to focus on each other.

Bwadu and Alia are tense. The tattoo of the orange leaf on Bwadu's temple twitches with every comment I make, and I can see she blames me for taking Scarla away. She might not know we're leaving tonight, but she's smart enough to see it coming soon. But no matter how hard I try, I can't summon any guilt. All my dreams are coming true. I'm finally returning to heaven and going with the woman I love.

The mortal I love. I might never get used to that, but I'm happy to spend eternity trying.

Mahari has a high brow and a warrior's stare, but it is softer tonight. She lost many good fighters in the Battle of Solren, but she has hope for the future, I can see it in the looseness of her muscles and the brightness of her eyes. She doesn't even have the dagger stuffed in her boot I've never seen her without.

Lazius shovels roasted pigeon with buttery vegetables into his mouth like he's never eaten before. His white-blond hair is pulled back in three braids, making his chiseled face stand out. He eats like a starved beggar, spilling droplets of tomato sauce on his cream tunic, but he's not drinking nearly as much stewed wine as I expected.

"Going easy on the booze, Lazius?"

He grins through a mouthful of ox cheese. "Gotta save something for after you whisk gigantor away. I'll prise my inner drunken angel out as soon as you leave. These guys'll have to peel me up off the marble floor." He's another smart one. He doesn't know we're leaving tonight, but he clearly knows our departure isn't far away.

Bwadu's voice is strong and clear. "If you drink yourself under the table, you'll stay under the table. I'm not picking you up from anywhere."

Mahari smiles softly, her ebony skin glowing, her mood much better than her sister's. "You've got too much now, Laz. Those angels will keep you too busy to drink."

A pang of guilt tries really hard to affect me. Lazius will be exposed and vulnerable after Scarla and I leave. No Inflict, little support. But he's resourceful, and I'm sure he'll find a solution.

Lazius raises a glass and sips but only swallows a tiny mouthful. "There's always time for wine."

The evening is pleasant but unending, and when it's finally time to whisk Scarla into my arms and fly north, my chest is light, and my pulse is fast.

My heart soars as high as my wings when we finally kiss our friends goodbye, telling them we're leaving for Malanox and taking to the night skies. This is Scarla's favorite time of day when the world is empty except for us, and the black sky is endless with possibility. It is a fitting time for her to leave her world.

We make Malanox before snowfall, and Scarla wriggles around in my arms. "Do you want to land for a quick rest? You must be getting tired."

Her weight in my arms is nothing. "I could fly forever." I think about it for a moment, then check in. "How far into the desert is the gate?"

"About a quarter of the way to Desert's Maw."

"So close." I can't believe I lived within a few miles of the gate I've been searching for my entire life. "The Elysian plains are a fucking desert?" The plains are said to border the gate to heaven, and I must admit, I expected flowers and grass, not endless sand.

I continue flying through the night, and the stars twinkle brilliantly above us as we land.

Scarla looks up at me, her eyes shining. "Can you see it?"

I can. The entrance to heaven, the way home. The Ring of Roth glows bright red on my finger, pulsing with the energy coming off the gate. I feel it too, like electricity sparking through my veins.

The gate is taller than the towers of Malanox Castle, with the wings of angels etched upon it, each pore and hair on their wings visible. The detail and craft are exquisite.

"Do you see the angels crafted into the gates?" I ask in wonder. I've never seen such beauty.

Scarla scans the gates, joy reflecting on her face. "I see runes and etchings, puzzles to solve."

Bliss bounces through me like an overexcited puppy. The gate tugs at me, pulling on something deep within me like a magnet for my soul. I take a few steps forward, clutching Scarla's hand, and she comes with me.

The yearning gets stronger as I approach the gate. Ten life-times' worth of dreams are about to come true. I'm returning to heaven, and I'm going with Scarla.

Without her, nothing is worthwhile.

I look at her face, which is glowing. She looks blissful and contemplative, wrapped in the green cloak that swallows her. I touch her warm hand, radiating heat like a campfire at night. Her skin is soft, smooth as velvet, and her eyes filled with emotion.

She kisses me softly. Her lips are sweet like berries. The taste lingers on my tongue minutes after we have broken away, both staring at the glowing gate.

It is the last kiss we will share on earth.

She tilts her head to look up at me, the otherworldy light of the gate reflecting an odd expression in her wide eyes. "Ready?"

"Ready." I step forward, her soft firm hand in mine, my soul reaching its epiphany as my body passes through the boundary between heaven and earth.

Bliss sweeps through me as I take the next step. The world is a white blur like I am being pushed through a snow tunnel lit with specks of red light like glowing embers.

Then I realize Scarla's hand is no longer in mine. I turn and see her guilty face stepping back on the earth side, away from the gate.

Her hands curl into fists, and she drops my gaze, then my heartbeat grows irregular, tapping unevenly in my chest.

I try to get back through the gate to her side, but my way is blocked.

I stare at her, shouting, but she can't hear me. She can't even see me because she is studying the sand, the gate, looking everywhere but at me.

Finally, she meets my eye, her chin quivering, a soundless word on her lips. "Sorry."

Scarla

I walk through the desert all night, the snow falling heavy and cold around me.

Tears burn my eyes as I think about Zaden, and the guilt weighs me down like an anvil, and a tightness squeezes my chest. I gripped his hands tightly and looked into his eyes, telling him we'd pass through the gate together—a lie I regret with every fiber of my being.

But the guilt will pass. The sadness will pass. It will feel fleeting with the benefit of hindsight.

I have unfinished business here on earth. Things I need to do, need to wrap up.

And I couldn't make him stay a moment longer. Whenever I looked at him, I saw hope glimmering in his eyes, and I knew he needed to return to heaven. I made my decision, and I'll live with it. But it feels like shit.

After hours of trudging through the thick snow, I finally arrive in Malanox. I head straight for the Undercity and smile as I approach the guards on duty.

I recognize Tone Perkins and smile wearily. "Hi, Tone."

He looks shocked at seeing me. "Scarla? Is that really you?"

I shrug. "How many copper-haired vestiges have you been flirting with, Tone?" If he doesn't know what a vestige is yet, he soon will.

He grins, and I feel less sad, almost happy. He was one of my friends, after all. I spent so long wishing I had more, but I should've looked around me and appreciated the ones I already had.

"Your grandma was remarkable," I say. Fra Perkins gave me Gaze after I watched over her death...her quiet, natural death.

He looks confused at the sudden change in topic. "Oh, thanks."

"She gave me a great gift, and I wish I could give it to you."

He looks confused again but lets me pass by without comment. I shoulder through the first set of heavy ox-hide curtains, and the temperature warms up considerably. My feet echo in the cavern, and I inhale deeply in the musty, dank underground air. A low whinny from the stables reaches my ears and startles me.

I stole Tone Perkins' inheritance. I never realized that before, but it's true. I don't know how Fra Perkins inherited it herself, whether she witnessed the death of an angel or, more likely, the death of a vestige with Gaze. It probably transmitted from generation to generation within the Perkins family, each person bearing witness to a parent's death and inheriting one of the rarest vestigial powers.

I feel a bit guilty that I stole it. That I witnessed Fra Perkins's death and ended up with Gaze. And I have no intention of dying peacefully in my sleep, which means Gaze will die with me.

With a quick glance back at Tone, I push through the second set of hanging ox-hide curtains, and the temperature inside the main cavern of the Undercity is deliciously warm. I unfurl and relax, soaking up the warmth. The cavern is smaller than I remember, though still large enough to contain Malanox castle.

Apart from being smaller, it looks just like the Undercity I remember from childhood, except now the black cave walls are lined with glowing trails, and some folks have a vestigial shine. I wander past the old folks' area and the creche, both quiet at this time of night. There's little sound except for the occasional chicken squawk and the echoing of my footsteps in the stone space.

A few people are standing around a snowmelt catch, chatting quietly. Dad is there, filling a mug with water and speaking with Pa Chen. He works nights and sleeps days and has done for as long as I remember.

His bushy beard is more gray than copper now, but his wild hair is still the same color as mine. His big brown eyes light up when he sees me, and he pulls me into a gruff, coal-scented hug. He must have been working the mines again.

"Scarla! You're okay." He holds the embrace a beat longer than he usually would. He's grown more affectionate the longer I've been away. "I was so worried about you." He pushes me to arm's length to inspect me, then pulls me close again. "There were rumors of a battle in Solren. Were you there?"

I hold him back. It feels good to be embraced by my dad. "Yes," I murmur into his coarse brown shoulder.

"Of course you were," he says, grinning.

I give him the rundown of events. How the resistance fighters of Desert's Maw crossed the desert to help us, how the warriors of Solren coordinated resources, how Leo acted as a spy, and how the battle went down.

By the time I finish my tale, half a dozen people are listening, and Dad's eyes shine. "You did all that? Berry, I'm so proud."

"I didn't do it alone. But I helped."

"And where's Leo?" He looks around like my childhood friend might be hiding behind me.

My eyes burn with tears, and the words catch in my throat, but I force them out. "Leo didn't make it. He sacrificed his life to save Zaden's."

Someone gasps, and another chokes out a sob. I scan the gathered night workers, cursing myself for not checking if Leo's family was among them. Thankfully, they're not. I'll have to break that news to them carefully.

Dad blanches. "Zaden?" That word is so laden between us. I was obsessed with Zaden for months after Leesa died, convinced he played a part in her death. It turned out I was right, but not how I'd thought.

I'm still obsessed with Zaden, even more so now. He is my everything. And the guilt at tricking him into leaving for heaven without me presses down on me again.

Dad doesn't miss my reaction to his name. "Are you okay, berry? Is Zaden okay?"

"Yes," I finally manage to say. "He's okay."

Dad pulls me into another hug, and I relax against him. It isn't quite the mountain lion cuddles I remember from my youth because I'm almost as tall as him now, but it is just as comforting.

"Zaden left Malanox castle," I say carefully, "for good." I can't bring myself to tell him the whole truth. That Zaden has left the earthly plane forever. "You can go live in the castle if you want, Dad."

He looks around, shrinking. "No, I'll stay here. Your mother...
"

Mom lived here in the Undercity. The stone walls are imprinted with memories of her. Is a part of Dad still waiting for her to return? Does he want to stay here so she knows where to find him?

My heart breaks for him. Mom is never coming home.

"I looked for her in Desert's Maw."

"Your mother?" Dad looks up sharply, his eyes focused, too much fucking hope in his face.

The onlookers melt away, leaving me and Dad alone, giving us some privacy. Folks in the Undercity are good at creating bubbles of solitude among the massive spaces and communal living.

Dad seems to stop breathing. "How is she? Did she mention me? Is she changing the world like we thought?"

It's on the tip of my tongue to rail against her, call her a bitch, tell him how she left for no good reason. But I don't want him to keep living his life waiting for her to return when I know damn well she won't.

The kindest thing is to lie. "Mom died, Dad. She lived for a while working as a performer to make other people happy." I go for a half-truth. "But she's dead. She's never coming back. I'm so sorry."

Dad nods and puts on a brave smile. Maybe he's a little relieved. "That's okay. Thank you for telling me."

Lies, betrayal, love. It's all so fucking complicated.

I spend the rest of the night with Dad, swapping tales and soaking up his love. I duck in on some of the other folks who were my friends, even if I didn't recognize them as friends while I lived here.

Fra Wang from the underwing pulls me into a hard hug when she sees me. She's on duty, like always, with her gray hair tugged into two severe braids and her resting scowl face.

She's tiny and wiry, and I have to lean down to cuddle her, grinning over her shoulder. "Ha! I knew I was useful here," I tease.

"Don't get above yourself, missy," she scolds, and I laugh.

I visit my old sleeping hub, then Leo's, where I spent so much time. I greet people, and I'm greeted so much more warmly than I expected that my heart melts.

Telling Leo's family what happened to him is the hardest part. I want to run away, but even more than that, I want to share his heroism with his family.

I can't hold back my tears as I explain what he did for me, what he did for Solren. Leo's mom sobs when I tell her, and his dad has glassy eyes and a fierce expression of pride.

It's too early to tell how their lives will be affected by Leo's death. By his absence, the part he played in overthrowing VanDyke, and all the momentous changes that are coming. But one thing is certain. Their lives will change. His death meant something.

Scarla

I walk up the grand steps outside VanDyke's palace, the new resistance HQ. Or Government House, as people have begun jokingly referring to it. I wonder if that name will stick.

I find Bwadu in the foyer, where gold and cream marble vie for attention. Those uncomfortable hard sofas are still here, but I doubt anyone has ever sat on them.

Bwadu is inspecting a bust carved from precious hardwood with a disgusted scowl. "I hate this place."

"Not enough ornaments for you?" I tease.

"Too many ornaments. Too much wasted wood. It's a fucking disgrace."

I grin. There is little risk of the general becoming a power-hungry despot and keeping all the riches for herself.

"Exactly right. You'll make a good leader," I tell her.

"We'll both make good leaders," she corrects, looking at me suspiciously. She must suspect I plan to go to heaven because every time I comment on the future, she rephrases whatever I say to put me front and center. I don't have the heart to admit the truth.

"Sure, that's what I meant. Have you seen Lazius?"

"What do you want with him?" She puts down the wooden head and gives me one of her filthiest fuck-off stares. I'm still in awe of her strength, her inner warrior, even though I am her equal now. But mine is manufactured, stolen from fate and death, but her power is innate.

"Secret angel business," I say cheekily.

"Stupid bloody angels," she mutters, and I can't help pulling her into a hug and planting a kiss on the curling orange-leaf tattoo on her temple.

She pushes me away and tells me Lazius is in the old servants' quarters, so I dive in and find him wandering along, allocating warriors to any empty rooms. It's incredible how many servants decided to stay, some to keep running the palace, others to do their part to help run the city. For those who left, their rooms are being reassigned.

The angel lingers in the doorway of a room with three beds, and I realize with shock it's the room where I was held captive. The last place I saw Molly.

"I thought I smelled you," he remarks without even turning his head. He wears a white shirt and tan pants, clean and crisp.

I sniff my underarms, but he misses the joke because he's still staring inside the room.

"Did you spend time in here?"

Wow, I had no idea human scent lingered for so long. I brush past him, enter the room, and sit on the middle bed, which was mine. The springs creak beneath me. "Yes. VanDyke kept me prisoner here. This is where I met Bwadu."

"So, this is where it all started."

"I guess." I ask him about the angels, the ones in the cells beneath Belial's palace.

A weary expression crosses his face. He was imprisoned for years in those very cells, and I can see he hates being the jailer. "Marlon and Wutan are still in the cells. We have angels round-the-clock watching them. But it's tiring, and I don't know how long I can keep it up."

I can see what it costs him to act the jailer, and I want to relieve his burden. "It would be easier if you had Inflict."

He laughs. "Yes. A thousand times easier."

I stare at him for a beat. "So take it."

His face is light when he looks at me as though I'm joking, his forehead smooth and his eyes sparking. "To take Inflict, I'd have to kill you. What will it be, gigantor? Strangulation or drowning?"

I shrug. "I'd prefer something less painful."

"Sure thing, one Angelfire death coming right up. I can't guarantee it's pain-free, but I can guarantee it's fast."

His golden-white hair is in three braids, and in his light clothes, he looks thoroughly angelic. He still thinks I'm joking, but I'm not.

Finally, he catches on. "Wait. Are you serious? I may be a drunken blithering fool, but I won't murder you. You have a lot of work to do here anyway. We can't run this place without you."

I hold his gaze. "Yes, you can."

"But don't you want to stick around and make sure things go smoothly? Make sure this cart stays on the road?"

I do. I yearn to stick around, play my part, and do everything I can to make sure this turns out well and see it through to the very end.

But I want Zaden more.

I shake my head. "I'd kill myself, Lazius, but that would be a waste. I need you to have Inflict so you can control the asshole angels. Will you do that for me? Will you kill me?"

He strides up and down the small room, pacing like his life

depends on it, running a hand over his tightly-braided hair. "Fuck-the-Maker, I don't want to. I won't do it. I don't want your stupid Inflict. I don't want to be the Cloaked King."

"That's why you will be so good at it. Besides, you won't have Gaze, so you'll only be half-king."

He scowls. "Fuck you, gigantor."

I grin. "Fuck you too." I stand up, cross to Molly's bed, and lie down, wishing I could smell her the way angels can. Maybe I'll see her soon. I close my eyes.

Am I ready to die? Not really. I don't think I ever will be. But I'm ready to see Zaden. In fact, I'm dying to see him.

"Do it now, Lazius. Please."

The angel grinds his jaw hard enough that I can hear his teeth crunching.

I open my eyes so I can meet my death head-on. It arrives with a glorious blaze of yellow-white Angelfire, which fills my body with electricity, then drops me into an abyss.

Scarla

I wake up in heaven. Heaven is not a boring white. It is definitely not dry-grass brown or black stone or red dirt, none of the shades of dullness that populated my life. It is filled with every imaginable shade of warm and inviting color, a mosaic of every sunset, every star in the night sky, and every raindrop that has ever fallen.

I am on a rolling green pasture, a verdant meadow with a long, slow hill dotted with flowers. Above me, the sky is intense blue, like a floating ocean. There is no pounding sun, no devastating heat, just a diffuse warmth that fills my body.

I'm wearing a pale yellow bodysuit made from a material that is lighter than air and softer than clouds and feels as though I'm not wearing anything at all.

Calm and joy surround me. I take a deep breath of the clean, refreshing air and inhale the scent of blooming flowers. The atmosphere is so clean and crisp, like drinking water from a snowmelt. It's so peaceful here, so different from the chaotic and stressful life back home. A nearby stream tinkles gently through the meadow, so I stroll along its banks.

At first, I hear nothing. Then there is a sound, like a humming whale song, a deep thrumming. As I walk, I feel a presence beside me and turn to see a man smiling at me. He looks familiar, like someone I've met, but I can't quite place him.

"Welcome to heaven."

He has dark brown hair and muscles upon muscles. His eyes glow a vibrant, intense green, and he's staring at me. He's wearing a simple white tunic and pants that seem to glow with their own light.

"Thank you," I reply, feeling a little shy in the presence of someone so perfect. His jaw is chiseled, his lips full, and the expression on his face is pure intimacy. I still can't place him, but a gnawing sense of familiarity tugs at my mind.

His voice is deep, rich, familiar. "You're welcome, mortal."

The song of heaven is a symphony of all the music I've ever heard. It is the rhythm of my heartbeat, my father's lullabies, the sound of Zaden's kiss.

"Zaden?" I ask tentatively, though I can't marry the name with the perfect being before me.

The male smiles benevolently. He looks every inch an angel, a shining piece of art. "Are you starting to remember?"

Memories invade my mind, rushing through me like a portal from another universe until I remember everything about my life and who I am.

I remember everything about this male.

His emerald eyes widen, and the crinkle around the corner of his mouth deepens. He pulls me into a hug, and my body melts in his arms as he whispers, "You came back to me."

"I never left you," I answer, stepping away from him.

"Well...you kind of did," he says with an amused smirk, so I nudge him playfully.

"Shhh. You're ruining the moment," I reply before leaning against him in an intimate embrace.

"When did you get here?" I ask after a few moments of

fleeting solace. He pulls away from me slightly, putting on a booming mystical voice as he says, "Time has no meaning in heaven, mortal."

His serious tone causes me to pause until I notice the playful twinkle in his eyes and can't help but grin. "So, like, two days ago?"

He nods with a smile and continues. "As far as I can tell, time runs the same here as on Earth and all the other planets."

My eyes widen in surprise. "Other planets?"

He frowns. "You didn't think Earth is the only one, did you? Or that yours was the only universe?"

"Well...I kind of did."

He tuts. "Foolish human."

I tut even louder. "Condescending angel."

We chuckle before returning to each other's arms, breathing each other in. His smell still reminds me of lilies of the forest, the flowers he always had on his bedside table. "Do you smell that way because that's how I want you to smell?" I ask. "Because that's how I remember you? Or do you actually smell like earth flowers somehow?"

He leans in to take in a long sniff of me while his face lights up with a radiant smile. "No idea. But I sure like the smell on you."

"So you don't have all the answers?"

He frowns seriously. "There's one fundamental question I don't have the answer to. But I need it. Now."

I tilt my head. "What's the question?"

"What do you taste like in heaven?"

He leans in silkily and kisses me. Cool, warm and hot. Each kiss is a mixture of all three. I taste his tongue and lips and breathe him in eagerly, feeling my body respond like it would on earth, but heightened. Heat pulses between my legs, a sensation that is both new and familiar. As we kiss, our bodies meld, and I feel a sense of completeness that I never knew was missing.

We break away for air, panting. "Wow," I whisper, grasping for words. "That was...amazing."

He grins, a wicked glint in his eye. "I'm just getting started."

We tumble to the ground but don't fall to the grass. Instead, the air catches us, letting us float around each other.

With just a thought, my bodysuit melts into nothing, leaving me completely naked in Zaden's arms. He gasps and looks me up and down hungrily.

We touch each other with wild abandon. All the shackles of earthly existence have been cast aside. Our bodies move together in a primal and tender dance, each touch igniting a fire that burns brighter and brighter.

He breaks the kiss and looks at me with smoldering eyes. "I missed you so much."

"I missed you too." My voice is husky with desire.

His hands roam over my body, exploring every inch of me, and I moan as his fingers reach my breasts. He teases my nipples, making me arch my back in pleasure. We rotate slowly in the air, floating above the grass, making gravity obey our wishes.

I reach down and run my hands over his muscular arms, feeling his strength and power. He breaks the kiss and pulls away from me slightly, looking into my eyes with a serious expression. "I want you, now," he says, his voice low and commanding.

I nod, my body trembling with desire. Every inch of me is alive, more alive than I ever was on Earth. His touch is fire, his body is silk, and his energy is coursing through his limbs and setting me alight.

"Why are you still dressed?" I grumble, and a moment later, his pants and tunic melt away, exposing his rocking fucking body, acres of muscle and toned skin that steals my breath.

We make love like we are outside of time, eternal. His cock is perfect, and my pussy is wet, and together we make one whole. We slide, thrust, and ride, coiling around each other, not even subject to gravity's whim but slaves only to each other.

My soul is singing, my heart is soaring, and my mind is exploding into a million pieces. He moans, and suddenly his cock fills me harder, deeper than ever, making me gasp. He holds still for a moment, and I kiss him, feeling his cock pulsing within me and shuddering as he comes. The pleasure is too much, and I come within seconds of him, our orgasms shaking the universe.

We roll apart, and gravity snaps on, tugging us into a heap on the soft grass, our limbs entwined, our hearts racing.

I run a hand down the loose muscle of his arm and play with his fingers. "Tell me you love me," I demand, turning the tables when he usually asks me.

He looks at me, his emerald eyes smoldering. "I love you," he says, his voice husky.

"I love you too." I feel complete. "And I hope you have an answer to your question."

He rolls onto his belly and runs a lazy hand down my arm, grinning. "I do. You taste like heaven."

I swat him aside. "That's a cop-out. Give me a real answer."

He doesn't even hesitate for a second. "You taste fucking perfect." He climbs to his feet and adjusts his clothing, then reaches out a hand." Now, would you like me to show you around?"

I accept his hand, and he yanks me to my feet. Excitement burns in my chest. "A tour of heaven? That's a definite yes." I look down at myself. "Er, do I have to do this naked? What does a chick have to do around here to find clothes?"

He slowly scans my naked form. "I don't think I want to tell you. I like you like this."

My hands fly to my hips. I watch as clothes layer Zaden's body, forming from a thought, and I try it on myself. I imagine a long swishy white dress that flutters around my ankles, and suddenly I'm wearing it. I laugh in delight. It looks like I have another superpower.

My chest flutters and dances, and my breath comes in short gasps. I skip a few steps, trying to take it all in, and scoop up Zaden's hand as we walk alongside the stream. "Is heaven all fields and flowers?"

He looks around. "Is this not pretty enough for you?" he teases.

"It's amazing. Beautiful. Extraordinary. I'm not complaining, just curious."

He grins. "There's more."

Beyond the stream is a collection of buildings. Each one is different, in various styles, creating a small village. Stone buildings, wooden buildings, barns, and what looks like a schoolhouse.

"That school looks interesting," I say, starting to move in that direction.

He tugs me back gently. "Not yet. Come on. I'm not ready to share you yet. First, let me show you where we live."

I can't argue with that. I'm excited to see what my house in heaven is like.

He leads me away into a glade of trees. We move slowly, the sunlight dappling the ground as we walk. After a while, he stops and points. "There," he says, beaming with pride.

I gasp. A two-story house made of wood and stone, framed by ancient trees and surrounded by lush gardens full of brightly colored flowers. On the balcony is an intricately carved wooden swing overlooking a sparkling pond filled with fish I don't recognize.

The house looks like something out of a fairytale—it's perfect in every detail, from the ivy creeping up its walls to the stained glass windows which reflect rainbow colors onto its steps.

I dash inside, taking everything in. It's filled with furniture crafted from real wood and adorned with pillows embroidered with gold thread. Bright rugs adorn the floors, and light spills in from every window, creating an airy, peaceful, inviting atmosphere.

Every room has its own unique charm. The bedroom is filled with soft sheets and romantic decorations, perfect for snuggling up in bed together after long days exploring this new world. The kitchen is stocked with every food imaginable, from exotic fruits to comforting dishes like roast chicken and sweet blyberries that remind me of home. Everywhere I look around the house, there are touches of love—dried flowers on picture frames, handmade quilts on beds—that immediately make it feel like home.

"We live here? We have all this just to ourselves?" I squeal.

"Yep."

I spin around. It's Maker-be-damned perfect. My very own above-ground house. "There aren't a bunch of folks just on the other side of the clouds who live in hovels, are there?" The only thing that could bring me down would be discovering inequity in heaven.

He beams. "Of course not. Heaven isn't a physical place, it's a psycho-emotional destination."

I scrunch my nose. "I have no idea what you're talking about."

He shrugs. "We have infinite space," he explains. "And infinite resources. Enough for everyone."

I wander into the kitchen and run a hand across the wooden counter. I sniff it and get a whiff of Rosen wood, the rarest and hardest wood available. At least on Earth.

A thought occurs to me. How does Zaden know so much about heaven? "Did you get all your memories back when you returned to heaven? Do you remember everything about your life before? Do you have a heaven-wife or something I need to worry about?"

He chuckles. "No heaven-wife. Just you."

I chew my lip, struggling to sort this out. "So you do remember everything that you knew before?"

Shit. Fuck. If he remembers everything, won't that drive a wedge between us? If he knows everything, I will appear foolish, separated from him by a vast and uncrossable chasm.

My heart races as dread creeps through me. He might love me now, but how long can that last? Will he ever find something in me that makes up for the fact I am clueless about the secrets of the universe?

He washes away my worries with a kiss. "I don't remember any of it, berry. You and I are going to figure everything out. Together."

My skin tingles with joy, and my heart is light. I breathe deeply, feeling the moment's stillness as a deep contentment washes over me. "Together." I like the sound of that.

* * *

Hi, I hope you enjoyed The Fallen Angels series!

Next for your TBR: Check out my series of fae royalty. Book one, A Court of Greed and Excess, features:

- Fae smut
- Found family
- Bully loves her
- One-night stand disaster
- Trials for the throne
- Touch her and die
- Enemies to lovers

As always with my books, there are bad men, badass women, and a beautiful but dangerous world.

Get A Court of Greed and Excess now!

Free Novella

If you'd like a FREE NOVELLA set in the same dangerous world of fae, sign up for my newsletter at zaradusk.com. It's a prequel novella set in the Realm of Caprice, where the weather is affected by the fae king's mood...and the king is NOT happy. A moody king, a badass heroine, and a beautiful but dangerous world—what's not to love?!

By signing up for my newsletter, you'll also get all the latest info about new releases, some character art, and other good stuff.

* * *

You can also follow me on Amazon, Facebook, TikTok, all the places. And I never say no to a good review.

xxx Zara